Praise for *The Royers of Renfrew – A Family Tapestry*

"...*The Royers of Renfrew – A Family Tapestry* painted an intricate, beautiful, accurate picture of what Pennsylvania German life would have been like in the 1800's ... You can relate to [the characters'] heartaches and struggles, their joy and youth, and the hard work they did every day to help their family survive... My mom and I took a trip to Renfrew after we read the book (my mom had read it too and loved it as much as I did) to see some of the places [the authors] mention... [the tannery] that Susan remarks was quite smelly...the ruins of the grist mill...the Fahnestock house...the four-square garden where, centuries ago, Rebecca and Susan knelt to plant and harvest their crops...

... I also learned a lot from the book, like that the family ate all of the hogs they killed including the brain!...I learned much about the Royer's culture, their family values, their faith in God, their hard-working family, and their lives...This is a book I would gladly read over and over again."

- Kiara Kalmey,
14-year-old student

"...Through times of both great tragedy and great joy, the family's values of faith, hard work, self-sufficiency, and personal responsibility offer stark contrast to the dependency of much of contemporary American culture. An absorbing and fascinating read that places our own lives in far greater perspective..."

- Donald Bruce Foster, MD
Author, *Kiss Tomorrow Goodbye*

"...I grew attached to the Royers and continued to think about them even as I finished with this marvelous story! An endearing story of childhood friendships, sibling rivalries and neighbors helping neighbors. I can't wait for the next installment."

- Sue Noreen

"...It reminded me of *Little House on the Prairie* but with a local flair...I hope there will be a sequel so I can find out what happens to these characters.

Also by Maxine Beck and Marie Lanser Beck

The Royers of Renfrew – A Family Tapestry

The Royers of Renfrew

Threads of Change

Maxine Beck and Marie Lanser Beck

Maxine Beck and Marie Lanser Beck

What the caterpillar calls the end of the world,
the master calls a butterfly.

- Richard Bach

This is a work of fiction. Though many aspects
are based on historical record, the work as a whole
is a product of the authors' imaginations.

Little Antietam Press, LLC

Published in the United States

Dedication

Dedicated to the staff and volunteers of Renfrew Institute for Cultural and Environmental Studies and Renfrew Museum and Park in grateful appreciation for their interpretation of, and care for the historic house and farmstead that were the inspiration for our story.

Acknowledgements

No work of fiction can ever see the light of day without the guidance, assistance, encouragement and loving attention freely given by family, friends and colleagues.

The Royers of Renfrew – The Threads of Change benefitted mightily from early readings by gifted editor Dennis Shaw. Thanks to Linda Zimmerman for her thoughtful editing of the manuscript, especially the German usage. Special appreciation to the staff of Renfrew Museum and Park and Renfrew Institute for Cultural and Environmental Studies who have been a constant source of assistance and encouragement every day. Stephen Beck has been invaluable in his role as business manager and advisor in the marketing of our books.

Photographer Andrew Gehman provided cover photography and Maxine Beck produced the interior illustrations. Thanks to Doris Goldman for sharing her expertise in plants of the Pennsylvania German Four-Square Garden and her creation of one of the shirts used on the cover photo. Special thanks to Donald Stoops for the loan of the authentic Pennsylvania rifle manufactured in Waynesburg (Waynesboro) by J.H. Johnston from the period and the accessories. Bradley Lehman generously loaned the black hats, so critical in the Brethren culture. Alex and Nick Zaruba, nephews and grandsons of the authors respectively served as worthy models for the front cover.

Any errors in our re-imagining of life on the Royer Farmstead are clearly our own. We hope our depiction of life two centuries ago will give visitors who wander Renfrew's 107 acres a better appreciation for the trials and triumphs of the Pennsylvania Germans who tamed a wild land in the quest for religious freedom and a livelihood for their families.

This book is a tribute to our Scotch-Irish heritage and our husbands' Pennsylvania German ancestors.

Maxine Beck and Marie Lanser Beck
Waynesboro, Pennsylvania
September, 2012

Authors' Notes

A Note on Religion

Religion played a major role in every aspect of the lives of Pietist Pennsylvania Germans who fled Europe to escape religious persecution. The Bible was the primary book governing their lives, and devotion to their principles and their community of believers was central to their daily lives. Children were given religious instruction in their homes from an early age and everything from the layout of the four-square garden to the religious holidays that determined the planting of crops was influenced by the dictates of their conservative Protestant sect.

A Note on Language

At the time of this narrative, the Royers would have spoken German exclusively in their home. But given their farmstead's role in the commerce of Waynesburg and the region, family members had contact with their English neighbors and needed to be able to communicate.

In addition, many newspapers and almanacs were published in German to cater to the many German settlers in the mid-Atlantic region. These publications were readily available to Daniel Royer and his family. Both the girls and boys in the Royer household were taught to read and write in German.

In this narrative, German phrases and expressions have been included to give the reader a sense of the sound and rhythm of the German spoken by the Royers and among the Pennsylvania Germans who, though most heavily concentrated in Pennsylvania, also settled in parts of Maryland and Virginia. These selected words and phrases are in italics to help the reader differentiate them from the rest of the text.

The Daniel Royer Family - 1814

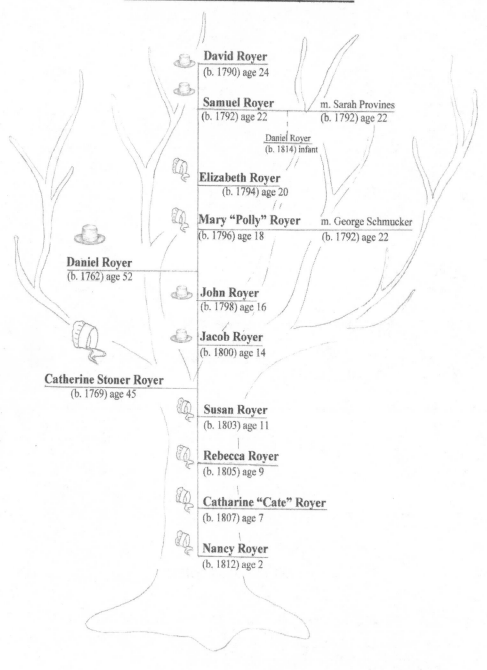

David Royer
(b. 1790) age 24

Samuel Royer
(b. 1792) age 22

m. Sarah Provines
(b. 1792) age 22

Daniel Royer
(b. 1814) infant

Elizabeth Royer
(b. 1794) age 20

Mary "Polly" Royer
(b. 1796) age 18

m. George Schmucker
(b. 1792) age 22

Daniel Royer
(b. 1762) age 52

John Royer
(b. 1798) age 16

Jacob Royer
(b. 1800) age 14

Catherine Stoner Royer
(b. 1769) age 45

Susan Royer
(b. 1803) age 11

Rebecca Royer
(b. 1805) age 9

Catharine "Cate" Royer
(b. 1807) age 7

Nancy Royer
(b. 1812) age 2

Contents

Autumn in the Valley

Eleven-year-old Susan leaned against the whitewashed pickets of the four-square garden fence watching her six-year-old sister Cate spin a tiny green and white striped long-necked gourd on the hard-packed dirt on the path next to the now-barren squash patch. Susan, thankful that the hot, humid summer days spent laboring in the garden were past, inhaled deeply the crisp, clean air. *I just love autumn,* she thought. *Not only is most of the harvest in and preserving done, but it's full of the fall gatherings.*

She smiled at her memory of the corn shucking at the Kneppers' barn the week before and in anticipation of the apple snitzen party in three weeks. "And next week, we'll all be at Samuel's wedding!" She couldn't help announcing this news to the countryside as she twirled around nearly tripping over the wooden corner of one of the garden's raised beds. Cate giggled at her sister's glee, squinting her deep brown eyes, a hallmark of everyone in the family.

Susan steadied herself and surveyed with satisfaction the nearly stripped 66 x 66-foot enclosed garden, the Royer family's main source of vegetables and herbs that she and Rebecca, her nine-year-old sister and best friend, had put to bed for the season. Every Pennsylvania German farm in this south-central part of Pennsylvania in the 1800s treasured these meticulously designed and groomed plots near their homes as part of the many other rigidly managed work areas that supported a thriving farmstead. The dictates of the German Almanac guided the planting cycles and placement. Not only did the neat rows and beds testify to a well-ordered household, but the garden's bounty nourished a healthy family and exemplified a thriving homestead.

Orange, green and golden vegetables that had been hiding under the mass of yellowing vines were piled nearby waiting to be hauled to the root cellar for storage. The small handcart parked at the center of the plot would soon be brimming with knotty gourds, ribbed pumpkins and the last of the red potatoes topped off by a few lingering heads of purple-edged cabbage and bulbous sweet potatoes.

Cate loaded the smaller vegetables, but with Rebecca's help the job would be complete in half the time. "Now where's Rebecca?" Susan asked Mukki, the family's golden spaniel, who had just chased some stray ducks out of the enclosure and sat panting victoriously next to her. The dog looked up at Susan as if to say, 'Do you want my help?' and dashed for the open gate to begin her search. Smiling, Susan flipped her long, light-brown braids behind her shoulders, snatched Cate's spinning top and took her hand. "Let's go look for Rebecca," she said. "I'll bet she's down by the creek taking her own sweet time getting here to help us."

Cate grabbed for one of the remaining large deep, red fuzzy plumes of the nearly five-foot high Love Lies Bleeding plant as they exited the garden. The chickens loved the seeds, but the fluffy flowers were beautiful decoration and great fun. She held some plumes to her forehead with a flourish. "Remember when John and Jacob used to stick these in their hats and march around pretending they were British soldiers?"

Susan nodded. "And look here." She took some of the feathery blooms from the tall stalk and held them against the back of her homespun skirt and began to strut. "It's fun to act like our old rooster, too." Cate followed suit and they shook  their 'tails' at each other squawking 'Cockadoodle-doo' and laughing.

As they ambled in search of their sister along the banks of the East Branch of the Antietam Creek that flowed through the Royer family farmstead, a brisk breeze set the ribbons of their small white bonnets flapping in the wind. The honking above heralded yet another flying vee of geese headed south for the winter to come. Susan gazed up at the vibrant rainbow foliage of maples and oaks sharply etched against the blue October sky. "Can't blame Rebecca for lingering. I forget from one fall to the next how glorious the valley is. It makes my heart pound and time stand still."

She lifted Cate closer to the towering trees. "Which one's your favorite?"

"The bright red ones," Cate said without hesitation.

"They *are* beautiful." Susan agreed. "But I'm partial to the yellow. The sugar maples always change first and lead the way for the rest."

"But the best *tasting* ones are right over there." Cate wriggled down and dashed toward the stand of apple trees at the north side of the garden. The yield had been so plentiful that John and Jacob had to prop up the heavily laden branches with wooden stakes to preserve the fruit until it ripened for picking. "Papa must have whipped the boughs really well last Good Friday to get so much fruit. I guess that superstition must be true," she said. After the harvest, the remaining apples would be pressed into cider, casked for vinegar, and boiled into apple butter, not to mention the dried apple slices that would go into pies and strudels to sweeten their winter meals.

"Look!" cried Cate pointing toward a bend in the stream a few yards ahead. "There's Rebecca. She's taking a nap."

"Shhhh!" Susan put her finger to her lips and gently pulled Cate to her. "Let's play a trick on Rebecca before we head back to work."

Cate quickly agreed and waited for instructions.

Rebecca was the soul of tranquility stretched across a large, flat limestone rock warmed by the sun next to the gurgling water. Her eyes were closed against the sun's rays. A pile of fallen leaves and the dark brown ringlets inside her white cap cushioned her head. Cate's voice had not alerted her.

Ever so quietly, Susan and Cate crept up behind Rebecca, the slight sound of their approach covered by the whoosh of the breeze through the treetops and the rush of the creek. Susan winked at Cate and delicately extended one of the reddish plumes over Rebecca's head. Then she lowered it and barely brushed the end of her sleeping sister's turned-up nose. Rebecca jerked her head and swept her hand across her face as Susan quickly withdrew the plant's wispy flower. Rebecca opened her eyes looking for the offending insect, but seeing nothing, closed them again.

Susan repeated the gesture as Cate stifled a giggle, but this time she drew the plume more deliberately across Rebecca's whole face. Rebecca sprang up in a panic to ward off the unwelcome intruder only to be met with her sisters' laughter. "You scared the life out of me," she grumbled snatching the bundle away from Susan.

Her sisters continued laughing and Rebecca retaliated by whipping the plants at them as they backed away.

Clouds of red fluff filled the air as the attack continued. Soon even Rebecca's sputtering anger transformed into good-natured laughter.

"We might have scared the life out of *you*," chuckled Susan fanning at the rosy flakes drifting in the air, "but just look what *you* did to the Love Lies Bleeding."

 The threesome soon headed back to the garden in a shower of falling windblown leaves. Cate was in the middle holding her sisters' hands and on every count of 'three' they lifted her off the ground and swung her a step ahead. After numerous repetitions, their arms began to tire. "Enough," said Susan. "Better save our strength for finishing the garden chores."

"Just one more," Cate pleaded.

Susan and Rebecca shrugged to each other and pronounced, "*Eins – Zwei – Drei*," dropped Cate's hands and took off at a run.

"Hey, that's not fair," Cate shouted after them. "Your legs are longer than mine."

6

The older girls spun around in tandem to wait. "And your *squeals* are *louder* than ours," Rebecca countered.

Hours later, the girls made their last sweep through the rows scouring the various garden beds to ensure that all the elusive vegetables were aboard the cart. They dragged the withering vines and stalks that remained through the garden gate to the compost pile by the barn. The cleanup had taken the remainder of the morning, but they extended the happy task as long as they could.

"I just hate to go inside. On a day like today, work is play. I feel sorry for the men cooped up in the mill and the tannery," Rebecca said.

Her sisters agreed, as Susan sighed. "But Mama needs more than Elizabeth and Polly to help with noon meal, what with all of the extra work she has to do for Samuel's wedding."

With a last look at the garden, she drank in a sweet draft of the day as they began pulling the overflowing cart the short distance toward the house. "I pray that the Lord will give them a day just as fair as this one," she whispered to the sky.

-2-

The Wedding

Seventeen-year-old Polly Royer sat among the large gathering of family and friends watching the young couple – her beloved brother, Samuel and his betrothed, Sarah, wearing a luminous white bridal modesty cape – recite their wedding vows. She squared her shoulders and concentrated all of her attention and prayer on the ceremony trying not to think about  her own nuptials to George Schmucker planned for the next year's wedding season. *Sarah looks so utterly happy – so beautiful*, Polly mused. *My mop of hair squeezed under my cap will never look as lovely as hers.* She sighed. *But I mustn't be so vain.* She looked at the groom's expression, anxious but alive with love for his bride. *Samuel's such a good brother. I'll miss him so, but his life with Sarah will bring him the blessings he deserves.*

Samuel's typically unruly shock of golden brown hair was coaxed into a smooth swatch that accentuated both his nearly six-foot frame and his soft brown eyes. The plain-cut black jacket rested stiffly on his brawny shoulders as he gently cradled Sarah's hands.

Sarah, her head slightly bowed, peeked up at Samuel with her soft, blue-green eyes. Her flaxen hair shone in a halo around her blushing face and in the tidy, flaxen bun at the nape of her neck. Though barely five-feet tall, she squared her shoulders with an obvious strength that belied her slight stature.

"Will you remain with each other until you are parted in death and taken to the Lord?" Deacon Myers asked Sarah Provines and Samuel Royer as they stood in front of the nearly 150 guests in the Provines' modest barn on the northwest boundary of Waynesburg, Pennsylvania. The gathering looked much like a typical Sunday Meeting of the Pennsylvania German Baptist Brethren. The only differences were that it was a *Thursday* and those who gathered shared *similar* prayers for the new couple rather than *individual* prayers about their private needs.

The Lord had blessed this new union with ample sunshine and robin's-egg blue skies this late morning in early November of 1813. As the service continued, a rectangle of sunlight streaming through the east-facing barn door retreated, signaling the approach of noonday. Many in the company drew deep breaths to help quiet fluttering stomachs and brimming eyes triggered by the vows – the elder generation recalling their own wedding days and the younger ones imagining their own exchanges of vows yet to come. Those less sentimental thought more about the food and festivities to follow.

Catherine Royer, seated in the front row on the right side of the center aisle with the women and girls, was parting with the first of her ten children. *Was it just 21 years ago that Samuel was born?* she pondered patting the restless knee of her youngest, two-year-old Nancy, fidgeting beside her on the wooden bench. *It won't be long until I'll be burping my first grandchild, God willing – and my own babe just out of diapers.* She felt a catch in her throat.

Daniel, her husband, sat in the front row left side of the center aisle. Striving hard to maintain a humble posture he thought, *Sarah's a fine woman for our Samuel – for any young man.* He recalled briefly the infatuation his eldest, as-yet-unmarried son David once had for Sarah. Thankfully troubles had passed without a significant break between his sons. *Sarah and Samuel have got a good start with provisions stored in their new cabin for the winter – and 20 of their 40 acres are sown with flax, corn and rye. Their four-square garden should be ready for spring vegetable planting,* Daniel determined, proud of his son's industry and preparation. *Still, it'll be hard to replace Samuel at the mill.*

David sat sourly beside his father. He had little patience for the trappings of weddings, especially when they occurred nearly every week between harvest and planting seasons. The brief twinge of envy at his brother's good fortune to have won such a comely bride took second place to his considerations of who to hire at the mill and for what wage. *Henry Lesher's done a fine job filling in while Samuel readied his new cabin, but he'll be expecting more wages to stay on than I care to offer. My hands are full enough with managing the tannery, so we have to hire someone reliable.* He considered his two younger brothers seated directly behind him – lanky, fair-haired 15-year-old John and stocky 13-year-old Jacob with his mass of dark curls. *It's a shame John's not a few years older. As it is, he and Jacob can help with the labor, but management responsibilities will have to wait.*

Deacon Myers' resonant voice drew David's attention as the ceremony continued. "Will you care for each other during adversity, affliction, sickness and weakness?"

Susan, seated behind her mother, squeezed Rebecca's left hand who, in turn, squeezed wide-eyed Cate's hand with her right. Susan's eyes burned with the tears she fought valiantly to suppress, unlike Rebecca whose bodice was speckled with the drops of her quiet, but unbridled weeping. As a muffled whimper escaped her, Susan winced inwardly. *I won't be such a baby as Rebecca*, she thought. *We should be happy for Samuel, not sorry for ourselves. I wish she'd control herself better, even if she's only nine.*

The eldest and most pious of the six Royer sisters sat soberly in front of Susan on the other side of little Nancy. Susan studied her 19-year-old sister. *Still, I can't ever be as solemn as Elizabeth. I know it's good to be at one with our Lord, but sometimes she's so focused on heaven that she misses the joy the Lord offers us here.*

With that thought, Susan noticed Samuel and Sarah turn to face the deacon and bow their heads as he took their hands in his. "Go forth in the Lord's name. You are now husband and wife."

Sarah Provines' family, especially her mother, had been planning and preparing for this day for nearly a year. After the emotional exchange of vows had come and gone, the monumental task of feeding and entertaining the crowd of well-wishers took center stage. The Provines' thriving cooperage business dictated an overly ample offering for their eldest daughter's wedding. Every farm for miles around boasted dozens of sturdy barrels and buckets that Ezra Provines and his workers crafted daily. Since the Royer family also owned a large, highly prosperous farmstead just outside of town, the union would favor both families.

Newlyweds Samuel and Sarah sat at the corner of two tables joined in an L-shape and laden with meats, bread stuffing, mashed potatoes, biscuits, coleslaw, applesauce, creamed celery and more. Vases of the leafy celery tops decorated the setting – a sign of fertility for the bridal couple. Hundreds of seeds from this year's crop would be planted in late summer on a quarter-acre of the Royer farmstead to ensure ample stalks for Polly and George's wedding the next year.

The unmarried young men rubbing their clean-shaven faces sat opposite the unmarried young women at the bridal couple's tables. Susan was thrilled to be included in this more mature group. Older married folks sat at other shared tables with those who were not yet married, recounting their livelier years as they watched the dynamics of the red-cheeked youth and the antics of their own adolescent children and toddlers.

". . . and my Opa painted the most beautiful angel on the front," Sarah Provines' sister Ruth told Susan as she passed the pitcher of gravy down the long table.

"It sounds lovely," said Susan pouring a healthy portion onto her bread stuffing and potatoes. "My sister Elizabeth has two angels on her *kist*, but it isn't nearly as full of linens and pots as Polly's. No wonder. Elizabeth doesn't think any men exist except for Papa and our brothers." She glanced at Elizabeth sitting at the far end of the table, serenely studying the fluttering bright yellow leaves of the maple branch just outside the barn.

Susan continued, "When Polly takes her *kist* to housekeeping next year, mine will take its place – the one I'll get on my twelfth birthday. Opa Stoner promised to have Reverend Lobach from Chambersburg paint the sun, moon, and stars on it. I can hardly wait." She couldn't help but picture Edward Lehman's golden-brown eyes sparkling in the sun when they had picked apples together earlier that week. Just then she heard his laugh above the chatter of the rest of the group, but she dared not glance in his direction and risk a telltale blush.

"Look, Susan," Rebecca squealed from behind as she tugged on Susan's sleeve and fumbled excitedly with a squirming lump gathered into the folds of her apron. Susan stiffened at the intrusion. As close as she and Rebecca had always been, lately her sister was just annoying, too babyish and demanding. Sometimes Rebecca's childishness was almost more than she could tolerate, as much as she tried to be patient.

Rebecca would have none of her sister's hesitation. When Susan ignored the pull at her elbow, Rebecca yanked her sister's forearm harder. The tug tipped a glob of applesauce from the spoon Susan was holding onto the table. Susan frowned and reddened. Ruth Provines giggled and turned from Susan to continue her conversation with the girl on her opposite side.

"Rebecca!" Susan snapped over her shoulder as she scurried to scoop the dollop back onto her plate before anyone else noticed. "Look what you've done, you silly girl."

"I'm not silly," Rebecca grumbled. "And I'm not sorry either. If you'd paid attention to me the first time, I wouldn't have had to pull so hard."

Susan swallowed her response rather than invite more attention. Taking a quiet deep breath, she forced a smile and turned around. "Now, what's so important that just couldn't wait?"

"Nothing," said Rebecca frowning as she drew the wriggling companion in her apron to her side, out of sight.

"Since when is nothing so hard to hold onto?" said Susan eying the obvious.

"Oh, this?" Rebecca acted puzzled and nodded at her side. "It's just a kitten – a *calico* – your favorite kind, I believe. That's all."

"Well, calico or not, animals don't belong at the table. I'm sure Frau Provines wouldn't appreciate you bringing her in here."

"Well, excuse me if I thought you'd like to see her. I've kept her in my apron so as not to upset anyone, but looks like the only one *upset* about it is *you*."

"Rebecca, come over here and stop bothering Susan," said their mother from a nearby table. "Cate just dashed out the barn door and I need you to fetch her before she finds trouble. Besides, you need to finish your dinner if you want your share from the cake table."

Rebecca eyed the table behind the bridal couple lined with sweets of all varieties – fruit and molasses pies, red velvet cake and iced yeast buns. The most elegant was the raisin-filled bride's cake, or course, but it was surrounded by other temptations like Mama's apple pandowdy and golden peach crisp. "Yes, Mama," she answered. She gave Susan a parting scowl and chased after her little sister.

Susan smiled a thank you at her mother and proceeded to work her way back into her conversation with Ruth.

By early afternoon only random slices and servings of the many sweet offerings remained as the womenfolk began the first cleanup of the day. The men would soon rearrange the benches for the afternoon singing and socializing.

"I don't think I can move," Jacob Royer groaned as he crossed his arms over his bulging stomach. His broad face, a common feature of the Royer men, flushed with the bloat of his earlier overindulgence.

"Me either," agreed his taller and leaner older brother and constant companion, John. "Glad we don't have to do farm chores today like some of the others. It'll be hard enough to move to join in the singing with those who stay on, much less haul wheat or pitch hay.

The whoops and hollers of the children who had been excused from duties to enjoy the festive day rang out amid the bustle of men rearranging tables and resetting new kegs of cider. With one meal over and another yet to come, the women made preparations for the late afternoon supper.

16

No child was idle given all the fun activities they had to choose from. The Provines' provided a wealth of metal barrel hoops for rolling with short sticks. Boys with pouches of their prized clay marbles knelt around gaming circles scratched in the dirt. Girls tossed flat stones at hopscotch patterns, and familiar rhymes accompanied the swinging jump ropes. Even Nellie Remmel, despite her limitations, sat beside the jumpers and clapped her pudgy hands a little out of time with the chanting girls.

Busy parents and older siblings kept watchful eyes on the children, but doubted that any temptation would be strong enough to draw the young ones away from the hub of activities. Only when the musicians began tuning their fiddles and banjos did Catherine Royer note Rebecca's absence. Child after child shook their head when she asked if they had seen her.

Breaking into the circle of older girls, a now-worried Catherine pulled Susan aside. "Nan's playing under the tree with Nellie Remmel, but I can't seem to find Rebecca. Do you have any idea where she might be?"

Susan instantly remembered her earlier tiff with Rebecca. She moved away from her friends thinking, *Best not tell Mama about it and worry her more.* "No, Mama," she said. "But she can't be far. I saw her not long ago over by the hopscotch squares. Don't worry, I'll find her."

"Well, let me know as soon as you do. I'll be in the kitchen helping *Frau* Provines finish up before the music and singing starts," said Catherine. "Rebecca's been so moody lately. Don't know what's gotten into her."

"I think she's upset about missing Samuel," said Susan recalling a good, sisterly conversation a week earlier when she and Rebecca were pulling up dead tomato stalks preparing the four-square-garden for winter.

"We'll all be missing his sweet smile, but she ought not to add to our worries this way. Off with you now, before she finds some mischief she's not looking for."

"Yes, Mama."

As Susan wove her way between the playing children, she remembered the kitten Rebecca had tried to show her. *Maybe she's in the loft of the wagon shed. Kittens love to play in the straw. That's it – the Provines' shed loft.* She dashed away toward the small structure not far from the barn.

Susan climbed the wooden ladder just far enough to peek into the Provines' small loft. At the far corner she heard the scuffle of straw and soft giggles. "Rebecca," she called softly, but held her place. The noise stopped, but no answer followed. "Rebecca, Mama's worried about you."

"I'm just fine," Rebecca snapped.

"May I come over there?" asked Susan. She waited. All she heard was the creaking of the shed's wooden beams. "May I, *please*?"

"Whatever you want," Rebecca finally relented.

Susan nestled in beside Rebecca who kept her back turned. Susan reached over to pet the kitten now curled into Rebecca's lap. "*Sie ist charmant,*" Susan said. No response. "I'm really sorry I didn't take notice earlier. You were sweet to want to share her with me, but I was busy talking to . . ."

"You're always too busy. *Du bist sehr gretsky.* Too busy to be nice to me lately."

Susan knew it was true and felt guilty, but had no excuse for why she had been so nasty. "You're right. I've been impatient with you and not very nice, but I'll try to do better. Things are so *vermengt* most of the time lately."

Rebecca handed her the kitten. "Everything's mixed up for me, too. But it's even harder when you don't want to be my friend anymore."

"Oh Rebecca, I'm still your friend – and you'll *always* be my favorite sister." They smiled at each other. "But, right now we need to let Mama know you're safe." She gathered the kitten into her skirt. "Besides, the musicians are warming up for the afternoon singing. You wouldn't want to miss that."

"Will you sit with me?" ventured Rebecca as they headed down the loft ladder.

"Of course. No one can sing *A Rose Tree* as well as we can."

"I know, but I like the tune better when we sing *Turkey in the Straw*," said Rebecca. "You remember, Samuel taught us the new lines last year."

Catherine spied the girls coming out of the shed. She happily waved to them and smiled, but then shook her finger at Rebecca. After Rebecca lowered her head to acknowledge she had misbehaved, the three shared a knowing look and Catherine returned to folding tablecloths.

"Let's go get a good place on the hay bales by the fiddlers," said Rebecca weaving her arm into Susan's.

"*Das ist eine gute Idee,*" Susan agreed.

They started toward the barn at the end where the musicians were setting up when Susan heard a familiar voice. "Susan . . . Susan?" Edward Lehman turned in his saddle having returned to the party after finishing his chores at home. It wasn't a short trip and required double-time with his work, but he had been determined.

Susan pulled up short to answer. "Well, Edward, you must have the fastest horse in the county – or else the easiest chores."

Edward was flattered that she had noted his absence and swift return. "'Yes,' to the horse, I hope – and 'no' to the chores." He held up one of his calloused hands. "For sure."

Rebecca looked up at her sister's glowing face and frowned. "Let's go, Susan." She yanked on her hand.

Susan, just as she had earlier that day at the table, ignored the tug and stayed focused on Edward. "My brothers' hands look like that, too. All the flax cutting and fence-mending. Hard work."

Edward smiled and turned his horse toward the hitching post by the barn. "You going to the singing?"

"She's going with *me*," declared Rebecca pulling Susan away from Edward.

Just as Susan was about to protest, John and Jacob passed by and patted Rebecca on the head. "Are you sure that's what Susan wants?" They laughed, smirking in Edward's direction.

Susan and Edward both blushed at the accusation.

"Yes!" Rebecca sputtered staring at Susan. "I'm her favorite sister and she's my best friend. Right, Susan?"

Susan hesitated as her brothers chuckled.

"Well, I'll – uh – see you there later, Susan," Edward stammered and rode away.

Rebecca puffed up her chest in triumph as Susan glared at John and Jacob. She barely resisted the urge to shake off Rebecca's hand. "Well, I hope the two of you are very happy. You're horrible." She stomped away dragging Rebecca behind her.

Jacob smiled broadly at their successful ribbing and nudged John with his elbow, but John appeared a little less smug. He couldn't help thinking about Ruthie Knepper's sweet, sparkling brown eyes. He sympathized with Edward, even though he hadn't dared share his feelings about Ruthie with anyone and risk making himself a target as well.

-3-

The New House

A multitude of stars and a crescent moon lit the sky on the subdued ride home from the Provines' house. The profile of the stately house where the Royers had lived for nearly two months waited formidably just past the stream at the end of their dirt lane. The new gray-stone dwelling loomed especially large in the dark despite the warm glow in the windows of the downstairs dining room from the large, softly glowing hearth that awaited them inside. To Susan, it still felt too grand, as if they were coming to visit a wealthy relative instead of coming home. To

Daniel, the large house was a visible measure of his success.

The four-bay, two-story home with four chimneys and new shutters resembled many of the prosperous farmhouses Daniel had seen on his trips to Philadelphia and Lancaster. He liked to think that substantial, well-constructed homes bespoke of God's blessings and the hard work of His faithful servants. At the risk of being prideful, Daniel smiled as he steered the team toward the barn, pleased to own a house that rivaled those in the East.

Actually, the Royers, with evidence of the farmstead's growing prosperity, were pushing some of the boundaries of their religion – a faith that valued modesty and 'plainness' above all else. Some of the most respected elders had grumbled at Sunday Meetings when the house was under construction about its size and the grandness of its deep-set windows that allowed the light to bounce across the high ceilings and plastered walls.

In no time at all, David, John and Jacob stored the empty cider barrels from the wedding party in the barn and brushed and watered the horses. The clank of pots and fire pokers and the scraping of the shovel on the limestone hearth as Catherine banked the fire to preserve some embers for the next morning, echoed through the walls. Every sound, down to the plop of hats and swish of shawls being hung on the pegs inside the back door and hobnailed shoes against wooden floorboards was much louder than usual in the absence of any conversation.

Samuel's wedding had ushered in a significant change in family dynamics that evoked a silent reverence from everyone. Although Samuel had moved into the small cabin he had built only two miles to the south nearly a month ago, when Sarah joined him, it would be his *home*. Now, she was his *first* family. Business as usual could resume tomorrow, but tonight was for each to say their own goodbyes to the first Royer to leave the fold.

Susan reached back for Cate's small hand as they made their way up the steep steps to the new bedroom they shared with Rebecca. As they moved down the hall between the four upstairs sleeping rooms, they heard the faint creaking to their right as Elizabeth abandoned the open Bible at her feet to rock Nan to sleep. Their eldest sister had loosened her dark hair from the strict knot she always wore. As the chestnut tresses cascaded over her shoulder, they darkly haloed her face and softened her usual somber expression. She hummed a hymn softly to Nan, a rambunctious toddler by day, but still small enough come nightfall to cuddle into a welcoming lap.

Polly had already donned her muslin nightgown and sat on the braided rag rug on the hardwood floor beside them surveying the contents of the colorfully decorated, oak *kist* crafted for her by her Opa Stoner. He would eventually build such a hope chest, for each of his granddaughters. *Polly must be taking stock of the household items she'll have when she's the bride – next year – moving into George's home,* thought Susan. She sighed and looked down the hallway. *This big house will feel perfectly empty before we know it.*

In the next room to the front of the house, David was bent over his small desk in the light of an oil lamp poring over some paperwork related to the family homestead businesses. No hint of quiet reflection tinged his typical stern expression. Happiness was a feeling he rarely permitted himself. John and Jacob were already sound asleep in their bed in the same room. Recently, John had developed a deep-throated snore, but Jacob and David had grown quite accustomed to the sound. Susan and Cate knew better than to disturb David with a '*Gute Nacht.*'

They ventured past their parents' room, the larger one facing the front of the house, and then back to their own doorway.

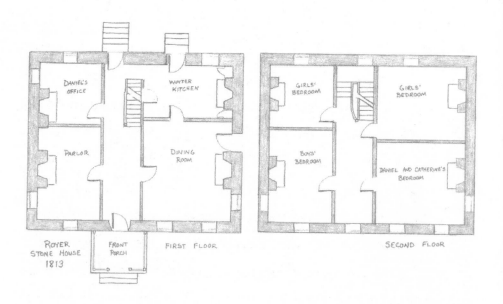

Rebecca was already snuggled under the featherbed in the bedstead that she and Susan shared.

"Shhh," Susan said looking at Cate and raising her finger to her lips. "Looks like the Sandman has already visited Rebecca."

They changed into their nightclothes and Cate settled onto her sleeping pallet by the wall as Susan slipped in beside Rebecca. Although Rebecca didn't move an inch, her breathing was too shallow for sleep and her shoulders were tense instead of relaxed into her pillow as usual. *Playing possum,* Susan determined. *She's probably still upset about Edward – jealous, I guess. I don't mean to hurt her feelings, but she'll just have to get over it. There's no reason I should have to choose between them.* Her heavy eyelids refused to stay open. *But, I'm too tired to think about that now. We'll have a good talk tomorrow.* She laid her hand on Rebecca's shoulder.

"*Süße Träume,*" Susan whispered.

"Sweet dreams to you, too," Rebecca answered softly and eased into her usual slumber.

Susan smiled and then fell asleep as well.

In the master bedroom, the parents were the last to settle in. Catherine stood beside the small hearth staring at the empty cradle. She couldn't bear to store it in the new attic even though Nan had outgrown it and no more little ones had arrived to take her place.

Daniel, usually a hard taskmaster, stood behind her and laid his hand on her shoulder. It was a gentle gesture reserved for their rare moments alone together. Catherine sighed. "It seems like only yesterday that Samuel was a babe, yet it probably won't be long until he has babes of his own." She turned to her husband wide-eyed. "Grandchildren, Daniel. Maybe one day soon, we'll be 'Oma' and 'Opa.'"

"God willing," he said taking her in his arms. "May He continue to bless us. Now, time for bed. The rooster won't crow any later tomorrow just because we want time to slow down."

Thanks to the early autumn rain, a healthy new growth of grass filled in the bare swath of ground behind the new house. The 24 x 24-foot dirt rectangle had marked the space where the log cabin that had sheltered their family for more than 20 years had previously stood. *Gut,* thought Susan as she made her way toward the chicken house to gather the morning's eggs, *the sooner the grass takes over, the sooner I can stop remembering our old cabin.*

The new house meant more room for their large family, an ample cellar for storage, a formal entryway and parlor, though understated so as not to appear prideful, and more. At times Susan dearly missed their small log cabin despite the vast comforts their new home offered. Wood shavings of the new construction lurked in corners and made her sneeze. The polished floorboards, though beautiful, squeaked constantly and sent chills up her spine.

During those first years of her growing up in the little cabin, she could practically hear the heartbeats of everyone in her family. All of her sisters except baby Nan, five of them, had slept jammed together in a small sleeping loft and the four brothers in another. There was never enough room to store everything required to sustain 12 people in so little space. The privy was practically the only place to be alone, and no one wanted to stay there longer than necessary. But the privacy and convenience provided by the multitude of thick walls and expansive rooms of the new house came with a price. Though it was sometimes nice to be *alone*, it wasn't nice to be *lonely*. And that's just the way Susan often felt since the move – especially at night, even though she still shared a bedroom.

'Give it time,' Mama had told her. 'It'll feel like home in time.' *How much time?* Susan wondered. *I hope it's not much longer.*

The heavy air of the morning amplified even distant sounds of the awakening Cumberland Valley. The rumble of a large supply wagon on the heavily traveled Baltimore Road that ran adjacent to the Royer property startled Susan and a few of the sparrows who had nested in for their winter stay. *Wagons already!* Susan thought as she made her way across the back yard. *They were still rumbling toward town when we bedded the horses last evening.* She shivered.

The more people talk about those awful Redcoats in Washington, the more 'ferhoodled' everyone gets. Seems like we don't get a minute's peace anymore, except at prayer. "And even when we're giving thanks, we're praying for the Lord to protect us all from what might come," she shared with Mukki, who pranced beside her. "It was bad enough when they were fighting in Canada. Now that they're so close, it's even worse."

When she opened the chicken house door, the dog scurried off toward the house to share some of the leavings from the breakfast to  come. Mukki would latch onto whichever of the men offered her a scrap of bacon and accompany him on daily tasks.

Many a sharp peck to her feet had made Susan wary of the cockaded rooster that pranced around the chicken house. She had just skirted past the strutting rooster to begin her egg-gathering when Rebecca burst through the door and startled the roosting chickens. A chorus of high-pitched cackling followed. Susan jumped nearly crushing the warm egg she was reaching for from one of the four nesting boxes arranged on the two-shelved rook opposite the dozen family hens perched on sassafras rods.

"Rebecca," she yelled. "Slow down. Don't you know better than to scare the chickens?" She immediately regretted her tone.

Rebecca hung her head and kicked a pile of straw. "I just came to help so we could get an early start to Samuel and Sarah's – to deliver the kneading trough, for good luck. You remember, don't you? Mama said we could go along if we finished our chores in time."

"I remember," Susan said trying to soften her voice. "Just take a deep breath. Don't have a conniption. That won't help anyone. We'll make it to Samuel's in due time, but first things first."

Rebecca stood silent. Despite Susan's attempts to mask her irritation, Rebecca still felt her older sister's annoyance. This angered Susan even further. *She's so 'empfindlich' – touchy about the least little thing. She takes everything I say the wrong way.*

"I just thought two could do the gathering faster than one," Rebecca mumbled.

"And just what are you going to gather with?" asked Susan. "Where's your basket?"

Caught in her error, Rebecca thrust out her chin at Susan. "You think you're so smart. Well, don't hold your breath waiting for me to help you again." She stomped off almost snagging her homespun skirt on the doorframe.

Susan shook her head. *Now why did I say that? I've got to stop letting her upset me so. She means well, but . . ."* Susan stared at the large gathering basket hanging from her arm. "There's plenty of room in this for all of the eggs. Aren't as many now with the colder weather. We could've shared this basket." *I've got to try harder.* "But she's so annoying," she told her favorite Redcap chicken. "It's not easy."

-4-

Busy Days

The steam rose from the bowls of corn mush and platter of Johnnycakes on the long wooden plank table opposite the large hearth. No formal blessing was given at breakfast because there was no common eating time. Every man, woman and child gave their own brief prayer of thanks as they grabbed what sustenance they could before getting a head start on the rising sun and the unending list of daily chores.

Daniel sat at the head of the table assigning the heavier of the farmstead's maintenance tasks. He lowered his tankard of cider and turned to David seated, as always, to his right. "Be quick as you can with the milling today. We lost valuable time yesterday and the orders are piling up."

David swallowed his mouthful of corn mush. "*Ja, Vater*. The orders from the army have added quite a burden. More hungry mouths to feed and less grain to sell them. It doesn't help that farmers and families are coming North away from the guns and chaos in Washington and Baltimore."

"It's putting a real strain on the tannery as well. Cavalry needs reins and boots and saddlebags if they have any hope of going against the British dragoons. They'll need as much leather as we can provide. I'll be missing your help at the tannery even more than before since you've temporarily taken over the mill for Samuel and George Schmucker has left the tannery to begin his carpenter's apprenticeship with his uncle."

"Samuel said he'd help out at the mill as he could, but we really need to find someone to take his place permanently. I've not had much luck in that area."

Daniel frowned. "I'm not surprised with so many of the able-bodied young men around here getting fired up about joining the fighting up North – signing up with the militias to fight the British *again*."

Elizabeth reached across the table to take away their empty dishes. "I pray nightly that the Lord will let this conflict end without more bloodshed."

Seated across from David, troubled 15-year-old John stretched out his long legs under the table and shook his head. Worry etched his long, chiseled face. "I heard in town yesterday that the Redcoats aren't content anymore to attack us from just Canada. As if the naval blockade at Baltimore isn't enough, they actually took over the port town of Hampton down in Virginia. They're coming at us from all sides."

Hearing no response, John continued cautiously, knowing he was treading on controversial ground. "I'm afraid the good Lord might be needing more help from us than our prayers."

Daniel's fist hit the table. "Enough!"

A gasp swept through the room. The only sound was the ticking of the Jacob Wolfe grandfather clock in the main hall. Everyone in the family was all too aware of the underlying tension between John and his father with the advent of this new war between America and Britain. David, sharing his father's opinion of non-involvement in the fighting, glared at his more radical younger brother.

Such unspoken brotherly arrogance spurred John on, in spite of the consequences. "Good men are putting their lives on the line for *our* country every day. It seems cowardly to just . . ."

Daniel swept his tankard off the table with the back of his hand. It banged against the backdoor just as 13-year-old Jacob was coming in from pre-dawn milking. He instinctively ducked behind the door for protection.

"Silence!" Daniel roared. "It is *not* cowardice to spurn violence against our fellow man. Those who live under this roof, who follow our belief, will *not* take up arms and will *not* let what *man says* overcome what *God decrees*. Do you hear me, John?"

John stayed respectfully silent.

Jacob, who was John's best friend as well as his brother, inched further into the room. *Say 'yes', John,* he willed his brother. *Don't push Papa on this – not now – not here. Just say 'yes.'*

As if sensing Jacob's wishes, John finally relented. "*Ja,* Papa." He dared not look for David's expression of triumph.

Jacob eased his stocky, but powerful form closer to John to offer support.

Daniel loomed over John. "Best you hear *and* remember. Our hard bought crops and leather goods support those men and their cause just as the cattle I drove to Valley Forge supported General Washington when he was fighting the British. The Royers owe apologies to no one. We will *not* speak of this again." Daniel walked deliberately past John and yanked his coat and wide-brimmed hat from the wall peg. "The tannery workers will be standing at the shop door by now. David, to the mill."

David took his place staunchly beside his father, his chest puffed up slightly under his work jacket, now even more confident of his status as the favorite son.

Allowing his father a head start, David turned to his younger brothers and added. "Best you inhale that mush and salt pork. Better work up an extra hard sweat today, if you know what's good for you."

The door slammed shut and Jacob caught John by the elbow as he lunged to snap at David's bait. "Let it go, John," Jacob whispered.

John shook him off, but stayed close. "I'll stay *only* because he *wants* me to go after him. But it's not over, Jacob." He looked at him and emphasized, "It's not over."

Jacob took a seat next to John. He grabbed a Johnnycake and dipped it in the dish of corncob molasses as the kitchen regained its normal hum of activity.

Catherine vigorously kneaded the dough one last time before shaping it into loaves for the baking oven beside the hearth. With each slap of the dough on the floured table she delivered instructions to her children. "Elizabeth, draw more cider into the pitchers for noon meal. Cate, you and Nan see to these dirty dishes and ready the ones for later. Polly, you can watch over the rest of the loaves baking in the oven while Susan and Rebecca and I deliver the dough tray to Samuel and Sarah. Jacob, make sure that it's secure in the wagon before you and John start working the flax. And John, I suggest you direct your frustration at breaking the stalks instead of breaking the peace of the family."

"Now," she turned to face her troops and placed her hands firmly on her hips. "Get to it. The sun's not shining just to warm the ground. 'This is the day the Lord has made.' Let's make good use of it."

The boys bounded out the door toward the flax break in the barn and Polly moved in beside her mother to begin dividing the large, yeasty lump into loaf-sized portions. "Oh, Mama. I worry every day that George will have the same thoughts as John about the Redcoats. But he doesn't have a papa set on keeping him home." Catherine patted Polly's hand. "Oh, Mama. What will I do if he leaves to fight? Papa would be angry and . . . and George might get himself wounded – or *never* come back."

"Don't fret over what *might* happen, daughter. We have enough worries keeping up with what *does* happen. George is a good man and you can only do your best to love and support him, whatever course he takes. For today, just make sure the bread's golden and not burnt when I get back.

"Pull a goodly handful of dough from that last loaf and roll it in some flour. We'll put that in the dough tray as a starter for Sarah's first loaves in her new cabin."

Catherine deftly managed the reins as Elsie, their sturdy mare, pulled the wagon up the dirt path winding past the neighboring Fahnestock barn to Samuel and

Sarah's new cabin on the 40 acres gifted them by Daniel and Catherine. The distinct nip in the cold air intensified as they reached the open expanse leading to the new home, but white smoke pouring from the chimney against a gray sky promised a cozy visit by the hearth.

"Get a firm hold on the dough tray," she directed Susan and Rebecca. "This last hill is steeper then the others." They reluctantly stopped hugging themselves against the cold and grasped the polished sides of the heavy 4 x 1-foot tapered box. Nearly every household had one of these – a sturdy top that doubled as work space while offering an enclosed compartment where the yeast could work its magic. After the dough had risen inside, the thick lid could be lifted off and used as a dough board for kneading. This was an essential item – a gift sure to be welcomed by the newlyweds.

As the wagon bed seesawed and followed the upward tilt of the road, the girls' muscles were strained to the limit. Hearing their grunting efforts, Catherine called back over her shoulder. "Not much further. Remember what Oma Stoner said, '*die Backmulde*' brings good luck into a new house.'"

Seconds later they passed the summit of the hill and the wagon leveled out. The precious wedding gift had survived. Susan and Rebecca relaxed and reveled in their success. The sight of Samuel's new cabin on the not-too-distant horizon made Susan yearn once more for her old cabin. Soon the familiar shutters and

 the beam above the front door with the carved, five-star *Hexefuß* that had once been part of the Royer family cabin came into view. *I hope the star's magic still works to keep evil spirits out of Samuel and Sarah's cabin. I wish our new house had one. I miss it,* thought Susan. *I wonder why Papa decided against putting one up this time.*

Catherine had no sooner reined Elsie to a halt than the cabin door flew open and Sarah bounded out wiping her hands on her apron. "*Willkommen*," she cheered. "I'm so happy to see you." Susan and Rebecca leapt out of the back as Sarah extended her hand to help Catherine down from the seat. "Come inside and warm yourselves. You must be chilled to the bone."

"Look, Sarah," Rebecca announced. "We've brought your new dough tray – for luck, you know."

"*Wunderbar!*" cried Sarah pointing Catherine toward the door and rushing back to look at the special gift. "*Wie schön!*" She climbed into the wagon and lifted the heavy lid. "And starter dough from Mutter Royer's delicious breads! Perfect. The loaves from our marriage offerings are nearly gone. Now I can bake my first bread in our very own kitchen. I have the ideal table stand for it, close to the hearth."

"Now don't try to lift it out yourself," Catherine advised from the cabin doorway. "Samuel can handle that later."

Soon the four were seated at the freshly hewn wooden plank table warming their hands around the tin cups of warm cider Sarah had flavored with a little nutmeg. Rebecca was dominating the conversation with her usual chatter that charmed Sarah and Catherine. Susan, having already heard most of Rebecca's tales on the trip over, sat quietly taking in the new cabin.

Everything's so crisp and clean – like a newly ironed dress, she mused. The spotless whitewashed walls evoked memories of the trip she and Rebecca had made less than a year earlier to fetch lime for the paint from the family kiln. She recalled Papa's very words, *'We'll need plenty if Sarah wants as much whitewash on their new cabin as Mama did on ours when we were first married.'* Susan recalled with a shiver Rebecca's falling through the ice of the stream by the kiln and the frightening moments until George rescued them. The broken arm she suffered that day still ached on cloudy days like today. She rubbed her forearm. *I wonder if our old cabin looked like this – this new – when Mama and Papa were young.* She looked across the table at her mother. *It's hard to imagine Mama and Papa ever being as young as Sarah and Samuel.*

So much of the cabin was a scrubbed version of the one that Susan had lived in up until their move to the new house just months before. *Was it really this tiny?* She studied the 24 x 24-foot area, the central hearth separating the kitchen from the rear sleeping alcove, the tiny iron stove fed by the fire's heat that helped warm the space. *That's our old stove,* she marveled. *It seems so small now, compared to our new five-plate cook stove.* She scuffed her feet softly across the packed-dirt floor. *And I forgot how hard the new wood floors felt when we first moved.*

She shifted her eyes up toward the rafters and the small lofts under each sloping eave. *We all used to sleep up there – except Mama and Papa and baby Nan! It all feels so long ago and far away.*

"The four-square garden's tilled and ready for spring planting and Samuel's making good progress on the barn," Sarah reported. "He hopes to finish before the weather gets too cold for the livestock. The chickens are already roosting in the far corner and I gathered five eggs just yesterday from the nesting box." Sarah's voice was full of enthusiasm and anticipation. "It's all so exciting, but . . ." she faltered. "It's so quiet when Samuel's out working. Not like Waynesburg where folks are buzzing around from sunup to sundown. I can't help but feel lonely sometimes – town life feels so far away, even if it's only a few miles." She frowned slightly, but quickly recovered. "I can't wait for Saturday's apple snitzen at the Newcomers'."

"Yes, the snitzen parties are always a good time," said Catherine. "Apples were plentiful this year. We have nearly 20 barrels of cider after just two pressings. Plenty for drinking *and* for vinegar. Jacob's set to deliver a barrel of sweet cider and three bushels of fresh apples to the Newcomers' barn tomorrow for our family's part in the festivities."

"I just love the smell of the hot cider and snitzen cooking down to yummy apple butter," said Rebecca licking her lips.

"But the most fun is the stirring," said Sarah winking at Susan. "Isn't that right, Susan?"

Susan blushed and shook her head trying to act unconcerned. "I suppose. Better than cutting the whole apples into snitz."

"I guess it all really depends on *who* your stirring stick partner turns out to be. I remember the first time Samuel and I shared the job." Sarah was clearly enjoying this gentle teasing. Catherine and Rebecca were an eager audience.

Susan ignored the comment and walked over to the window. *I can't believe she's saying this in front of Mama and Rebecca. Stop it, Sarah.* Pushing aside the homespun curtain she said, "Looks like it might start raining soon. I hope Samuel gets back in time to unload the dough tray before it gets wet."

Catherine sensed Susan's unease and widened her eyes at Sarah. Sarah understood her expression and moved toward the door changing the subject of conversation. "I'd love to show you our new garden and barn. Maybe we'll find Samuel there and ask him to take a break and move the dough tray inside. If not, I'm sure the four of us could easily manage. Besides, Samuel would be sorry to miss seeing you."

At the mention of seeing her favorite brother, Rebecca swooped outside like a hawk after a rabbit.

Gut, Susan thought, sighing in relief. *Enough talk of snitzen parties.* "Wait for me, Rebecca," she called taking off after her sister.

Catherine came to Sarah's side. "Those two girls are a real challenge right now. Like two peas in a pod one day and lard and vinegar the next."

"I don't see how you keep all of your children straight," Sarah marveled. "So many to care for and each one so different. But enough about my news, tell me about *your* new house – and the wedding plans! Polly must be *so aufgeregt.*"

"Oh she's barely able to keep her wits about her most days. Honestly, Sarah, they are *all* growing and changing so fast. This snitzen party could have more folks than Susan fretting about who will be stirring which kettle. Seems as though you and Samuel are just the start of things to come."

-5-

The Snitzen Party

"*Oh, das fühlt mir so gut!*" said Susan as she eased her bare backside a bit closer to the crackling fire. Rebecca soaked in the soapy, warm water lapping around the edges of the large washtub a few feet in front of her. The smell of lye and chamomile saturated the humid air. Having relished the last wave of heat from the hearth, Susan secured her grip on the linen towel wrapped around her scrubbed body. She made her way to her clean clothes hanging on the wooden pegs near the door of the new summer kitchen. Raising her arms, she ducked under the hem of her homespun slip and wiggled to urge the garment to fall into place.

"I think *das Sommerhaus* is my favorite part of the new house. It's soooo nice to take our time with a bath and not have to wait  'til the menfolk are out and rush around all shivery and *ferhoodled,*" she said. "Even if we only get a chance every few months."

"Me, too, Schwester," Rebecca agreed. "And it's soooo nice to have the heat and stink of candle and soap making out of the house. But I do miss the smell of fresh bread when Mama bakes out here in the spring and summer, although it keeps the big house from feeling like *we're* baking in an oven."

"Now that the tannery workers take their meals in here, the stink of the hides stays out of the house. The windows catch such a nice cross breeze when they're open and it's easy to freshen the air." Susan drew a deep breath.

Rebecca pinched her eyes shut and lowered her head under the tepid water, her dark curls spreading like a fan on the rippling surface as Susan secured the waist of her ankle-length skirt over her bodice. Suddenly, Rebecca emerged expelling a loud hiss and brushing her wet eyelids. Susan picked the damp, linen towel from the peg and moved to the tub holding it like a curtain for Rebecca. Rebecca twirled herself into the suspended cloth and dashed to where Susan had stood by the fire just moments earlier. "It feels so good to be clean," she said. "Especially with the snitzen party happening tomorrow."

Susan felt the same way but didn't respond, considering it better to avoid the subject since she couldn't stop thinking about stirring the kettle with Edward Lehman. Rebecca always got *gretzy* if his name was mentioned. *She's such a 'Säugling' about it,* Susan thought, feeling so much wiser than her younger sister. "It feels good to be clean anytime, silly. Now get dressed before John and

Jacob get so tired of waiting their turn that they burst through the door."

After both girls were dressed and ready to relinquish the summer kitchen to the next bathers, Susan draped the wet towel over one of the rope clotheslines strung in a corner. "Washing clothes is so much easier in cold weather now. I used to hate *Waschtag* every Monday, especially when the weather turns colder."

"Remember how the wet clothes would freeze stiff as boards on the lines and bushes outside?" Rebecca said.

"Yes, and our clean aprons used to crack when we folded them into the basket to bring them inside," Susan added. "It's even better to hang them in the attic of the new house in the winter. Have you noticed how the clothes sometimes take on the sweet smell of the dried apples hanging beside them?"

"Well, the Newcomers' barn is going to smell like a whole orchard tomorrow." Rebecca smiled and grabbed the door latch. "Ready to make a run for the house?"

"Last one there's a rotten egg," Susan laughed hopping in front of Rebecca and speeding toward the stone house only 20 yards away. "And don't forget to close the door, or John and Jacob will skin you alive," she yelled back.

The additional rooms of the new house offered more light, more space and more air, but the high-ceilinged rooms required extra maintenance. One large hearth and an iron heating stove had once been enough to warm their entire cabin, but now they had to tend seven fireplaces. John and Jacob were responsible for keeping the woodpiles stocked, but Polly, Susan and Rebecca were charged with tending the fireplaces. Even Cate and Nan were not too young to haul bundles of kindling upstairs.

Everyone in the family had hurried through their various duties this Saturday to allow time to prepare for the trip to the Newcomers' snitzen party. Rebecca was dressed and ready, as were the others, when she remembered that it was her turn to clean the small hearth in the bedroom she shared with Susan and Cate. *Ach du Lieber!* she thought in a panic. *Mama won't let us leave until all the chores are finished.* She ran her hands over her clean clothes. *And now the ashes and soot might get all over my dress.*

Most of the children had already gathered in the dining room awaiting the word from their parents to board the wagons. Rebecca studied their eager faces. *They'll be so angry if they have to wait for me. I've got to hurry before they notice.* She sped up the stairs to her room, shoveled the cold ashes of the previous night into a tin bucket, threw a few handfuls of tinder and wood between the andirons for that night's fire and rushed toward the door. Holding the dirty bucket a safe distance from her clean clothes, she whipped around the door into the hall and smashed into Susan.

"*Gott im Himmel*," Susan squealed as the ashes and soot from the upturned bucket exploded into the air and covered her freshly-ironed skirt and bodice. Rebecca fell back on her bottom and somehow avoided the worst of the mess. Susan stared unbelieving at her ruined outfit and glared at her sister who didn't have a speck of soot on her. "*Du bist ein Dummkopf!* Just look at what you've done."

Rebecca scrambled up and began frantically brushing Susan's skirt which only made the charcoal streaks worse. Most of the ash might have shaken off, but Rebecca's frantic rubbing smeared the dirt more deeply into the cloth folds.

Susan pushed her away. "Stop! Now it's really ruined. I can't go to apple snitzen like this." Tears of anger and disappointment started in dark rivulets down her cheeks. "I'll have to change into my old clothes. We'll be late. They'll already be stirring the kettles 'til we get there." She sobbed and threw up her hands. "And me wearing my old, wrinkled clothes." She scowled at Rebecca cowering against the wall and crying.

"Get away from me. You always ruin everything." Susan pushed past her into the bedroom and slammed the door rattling the framed samplers hanging on the wall.

Rebecca hung her head and didn't move.

"What's happening up there?" Polly shouted from the foot of the stairs.

"I . . . I . . . ," Rebecca stammered, but was unable to answer.

Polly appeared on the stair landing, took one look at Rebecca seated among the debris and immediately understood. "Oh no, Rebecca. Not today of all days. Where's Susan?"

Rebecca tipped her head toward the bedroom door and Polly lifted her skirt moving past Rebecca toward the bedroom to aid her distraught sister. Rebecca sighed between sobs. "I didn't mean to, Polly. Honest. It was an accident. It . . ."

"Just clean up the mess out here and I'll try to clean up the mess you made of Susan," Polly instructed. Rebecca just hung her head again. "Hurry," Polly sighed. "Pouting won't help anything and Papa and John just pulled the wagons up to the house."

Daniel Royer drove the lead wagon at a hurried trot. John followed in the second cart as they headed toward the Newcomers' farm. Papa hadn't asked the reason for the delay – he didn't abide excuses. A man of supreme practicality and purpose, he simply drove the horses past their usual pace to make up for lost time. The passengers endured the intense jostling without complaint knowing well their father's mindset. Catherine gripped the wooden board of the seat she shared with her husband. "It could take some time to tighten up the bolts on this wagon if we keep up this pace," she mentioned without directly addressing Daniel. Not immediately, but within a few minutes, as if to suggest it was his own idea, Daniel reined in the horses to slow down just a bit.

Abandoning her usual seat beside Rebecca in the bed of John's wagon, Susan burrowed into the corner furthest from her sister and stared at the bits of straw under her feet. She could imagine the expression she would see on Rebecca's face if she even deigned to look at her. *So she's sorry – so what?* she thought. *So it was an accident – so what? If she hadn't forgotten her chores . . . if she hadn't been so 'doppish' . . . if she . . .* Then the bumping of the wagon lessened and Susan's anger eased as well. *'To forgive is divine.' I know . . . I know I truly hurt her feelings, but . . .* Just as she was about to raise her head to speak to Rebecca, the unmistakable essence of sweet apple cider washed over the wagon and flooded all thoughts of forgiveness out of her mind. *We're nearly there!* She craned her head over the side of the wagon as dozens upon dozens of wagons, black hats and bonnets came into view.

The weather was unusually fine for November. The air chilled the nostrils a bit, but the sun wrapped everyone and everything in its warm embrace. Such a fine day allowed the gathering to take place outside. Vapor clouds of condensation hovered above four copper kettles collected from surrounding farms

 that were hanging under beech trees in the level area between the barn and the smokehouse. The cider had been boiled down the evening before with great stumps of trees fueling the constant fires. The labor for today's snitzen party called for constant stirring of the kettles as additional sliced apples, the 'snitz,' were added to the liquid. If the thickening mixture scorched the bottom of the pot, the apple butter would taste burnt and the kettle would require tedious scrubbing. The process took hours, but the work was made lighter by assigning it to the older youth and young adult singles. A boy and girl would take hold of the long handle of each of the wooden stirrers and move together in a circular motion until their arms got tired and others would take over for them.

Mama had agreed that Susan could assist with the 'stirrin' in' for the first time this year. Her stomach churned mightily with excitement and fear of embarrassment. Many a romance had sprung up with the apple butter steam, so the anticipation of who would share the labor and the laughter was on everybody's mind. Brothers John and Jacob would be in the mix as well, though they had the experience of past years to lessen their anxiety.

The Royer wagons were the last to arrive as they pulled in beside the others parked in front of the Newcomers' modest two-story log house. The family, minus David who had decided to 'stay home and do some *real* work,' disembarked and scanned the scene to determine their place in the proceedings. Daniel heaved a crate of empty, two-quart crocks crafted by Catherine's favorite local potter, John Bell, from the wagon bed. They would eventually hold their family's share of the apple butter that day. By the end of the day, they would take their place in the attic with the hard soap, cider kegs and strings of dried apples and cherries.

"Here, let me help you, Papa," came a familiar voice as Samuel rounded the corner of the house. "As I recall, you usually bring two crates of jars to apple snitzen."

"You remember well, son, but then you've not been gone from home that long," Daniel said putting his burden on the ground and sharing the kiss of brotherhood with his second born.

As Samuel retrieved the remaining box, he smiled at the others. "Sarah's been waiting to see you. She's in the kitchen paring apples." Polly immediately headed in that direction anxious to continue talk of weddings and 'going to housekeeping.'

Catherine watched her speed away and began assignments. "Rebecca and Cate, you follow Polly to help with the cooking and to cut and deliver snitzen to the kettles." Rebecca tried in vain to catch Susan's eye before leaving. *She doesn't even know I'm alive. All she cares about is that old Edward.* Her lower lip hung over her chin as she took Cate's hand and moved away.

Elizabeth stood quietly balancing Nan on her hip. Catherine looked at her oldest daughter marveling at her soothing way with children. "Elizabeth, I'm sure there are plenty of *Kindlein* that need tending while their mamas work, unless you want to join Susan and the boys at the stirrin'."

"Looks like they have plenty of folks there, Mama," Elizabeth replied looking toward the grove. "I'll wait for you *im Sommerhaus.*"

John and Jacob headed immediately toward the crowd under the beech trees. Catherine watched them leaving. *John's nearly a head taller than Jacob,* she mused. *It's good that he has Opa Stoner's height so I can tell them apart at a distance.*

Then shots rang out from the other side of the barn. "Sounds like the shooting contests have started," Daniel said lifting the crate from the ground and joining Samuel. "Let's deliver these and then go demonstrate how the Royer men handle a Pennsylvania rifle."

Gathering her basket with offerings of pumpernickel bread, sweet pickles and her favorite paring tools from under the wagon seat, Catherine noticed Susan standing alone tight against the far side of the wagon staring at the bubbling kettles. *Best I leave her to her thoughts. Not an easy thing, this growing up. I'll have a look later to see how she's doing.* She spied the Lehmans' wagon and horses tied up nearby. *Pretty sure the one she's interested in is here. That's who she's looking for – him and his stirrin' partner.* She patted her daughter's cheek. "You'll be fine, Susan. I'm sure some girl's arms are aching by now. You'll find a place."

Susan sighed and squared her shoulders thinking. *If I smile enough maybe no one will notice my old clothes.* She had inherited this longer skirt, to suit her age, from among those Polly had outgrown. Stubborn stains from spilled red beet juice and butchering days had faded, but their marks still mottled the linsey-woolsey. However, the many years of wear gave it a softer look as it fell in gentle pleats inches above her ankles. She smoothed her front, checked her bonnet and pasted a smile on her face, determined to enjoy the day. *Need to make my 'insides' make up for my 'outsides.'*

John's arrival at the beech grove proved very timely as Ruthie Knepper's partner had just developed a cramp in his wrist. John had been thinking about Ruthie's dimples and deep brown eyes for weeks and jumped at the chance to take his turn at the paddle.

Jacob was leaning against the gray bark of a nearby beech tree waiting for another place to open. He hoped the seat opposite Hannah Knepper, Ruthie's younger sister, would be the next one available. He lifted his hat and drew his open hand through his shock of dark-brown curls. Hannah's hair, even darker than his, glistened with sweat in the streak of sunshine peeping through the thinning canopy of leaves.

The closer Susan got to the hardworking group of young singles, the more certain she was that she had never seen the girl who was stirring the far kettle with Edward. *I'm sure I'd remember hair that curly and that red.* She continued to steal glances at the profile of Edward's partner as she greeted friends seated on stools at opposite sides of the kettles. Everyone was in constant motion to keep the tempering apple mixture from burning. *And her cap isn't like ours. She must be from up North. She's pretty and probably closer to Edward's age than I am.*

Susan edged her way toward Edward's field of vision when she heard her name.

"Susan," called Constance Newcomer yet again from her station at the kettle nearest the log house. Susan was so distracted she'd failed to hear her name the first time.

Barely disguising her reluctance to stop, she turned and answered, "Yes, Constance?"

"I'm so glad to see you, Susan," she said. "We were worried that something happened to keep your family from coming."

"Just some last minute delays," Susan explained noticing that Constance's stirring partner was as unknown to her as Edward's coworker. *Who's this?* she wondered. The high stiff collar of his jacket was also in the style favored by their more Northern Brethren – like that of the new girl working with Edward. Susan looked at Constance. "It would have been awful to miss apple snitzen on such a beautiful day."

"Susan, this is my cousin Jonas Eshleman from Carlisle. He and his sister, Rachael, who's over there with Edward Lehman, are here for my brother's wedding next Tuesday." She nodded toward the far couple.

Susan glanced in the direction Constance indicated, but spun back to avoid appearing overly concerned. She tipped her head at Jonas. "It's a pleasure to meet you, Jonas. My brother, Samuel was married just a few weeks ago. Weddings are a wonderful reason for family members and friends to get together."

Jonas' blue eyes flashed. "And what luck to be able to share an apple snitzen party during our visit – and to meet so many new folks."

"Susan, my mama just called from the cabin," Constance said stepping away from her place. "Would you like to take over for me while I run to see what she needs?"

"Of course," Susan fibbed thinking, *but what about Edward? What if his partner gets tired and I'm not there?* She wrapped her hands around the stir stick directly under Jonas' hands and sat.

Then *Herr* Newcomer's father appeared carrying an empty apple box. He turned the crate upside down on the ground and stood on top of it, coughing loudly to command everyone's attention. When conversations stopped and all eyes were on him, he announced, "On such a glorious day as the Lord has given us to come together and transform his gift of fruit into delicious apple

butter – on this bountiful apple snitzen day, I offer you a poem my
papa shared with me many years ago."

Then in low, resonant tones, he began.

"Who loved not cider-making day,
Across a tugged bench, astride
A busy, artless, rustic sits
To linger round the press and mill
And pares the apples for the rest,
And help the bulky barrels fill.
Who, mid the music, song, and jest
Or on the spring-wagon tongue,
Now cuts the apples into snits;
With rustic girk, the tongue astride,
While two by two, well-paired, by turns
Enjoy the mimic tomboy-ride
Lest the boiling butter burns.

A respite from severer toils –
Good butter must be slowly boiled;
To children always sweet and new;
According to the old-time way;
To older folks, it was a day
And so they boiled and stirred it slow,
Of neither work, nor yet of play;
Until the cocks began to crow,
A something rather 'twixt the two;
And e'en the horses seemed to know
And dance went on, and seldom ceased,
That lazily, they, too, might go.
'Til rosy morn adorned the East.

And now, the butter-boiling came-
Before they took the kettle off
That set the rural hearts ablaze-

They stirred the fragrant spices in;
That came as sure as autumn came;
And then with ladle, tin, or gourd,
Would that it yet came all the same
The boiling mass was dipped and poured,
As in those dreamy autumn days-
Amid the noisy clang and din,
With diffle, frolic, dance and play,
From copper-kettle, burning hot,
. . . "

The stirring had not stopped once during the recitation lest the butter burn, but everyone let loose of the sticks long enough to applaud the performance. *Großvater* Newcomer nodded modestly, his white beard moving up and down in appreciation.

As suddenly as conversation had ceased, its cheerful hum resumed. To Susan's surprise, Jonas proved to be fine company. Still, she kept a subtle yet constant check on the progress at the kettle shared by his sister and Edward. On her third glance to that purpose, she saw Rebecca adding a bowl of snitz to their station. Their eyes met before Susan could stop herself and she infused all of her impatience and frustration at not being with Edward into a scowl directed at her sister. Rebecca nearly dropped the wooden bowl into the mix. Edward grabbed it. "Watch out there, Rebecca. We don't want splinters in the apple butter." He smiled at Rebecca as Jonas' sister giggled.

"I'm sorry," Rebecca cried with entirely too much emotion for the situation. Edward looked at her teary eyes, saw she was staring over at Susan and realized the apology was more for her sister than for him. She pulled the wooden bowl to her chest and ran. Susan caught Edward's puzzled expression and turned away mortified. *Dear Lord! What'll I say if he asks me what's wrong?*

"Are you feeling all right?" asked Jonas.

"I'm fine," she said with an over-animated smile in case Edward was still watching. "It's just that my little sister sometimes makes me crazy."

Jonas pulled the stick in his direction. "I know how you feel. My little brothers are as pesky as horseflies sometimes."

One by one the kettle workers were excused. The apple butter concoction was deemed ready if it no longer 'wept out' around the edges, but formed a simple heap when spooned onto a small dish. After hours of stirring, it was time to fill the waiting jars and let the sweet treat cool. All who had come for the day had eaten their fill of good food at various times as their work allowed and they now loaded their wagons for the ride home.

The men moved the empty kettles to the barn for cleaning and doused the fires as the women placed the last of *Frau* Newcomer's dishes on her kitchen shelves and gathered the family belongings and their children.

"Has anyone seen Rebecca?" asked Catherine as the group of remaining guests continued to assemble around the cabin area. "Rebecca!" she called again as she had been for nearly ten minutes.

A chorus of 'no's' and questioning looks offered no answer. As word of Catherine's concern spread, more and more folks huddled around the wagon. A missing child was serious business, especially with daylight nearly gone.

Daniel took his rifle from under the wagon bench and announced. "All men who are willing, check the grounds and perimeter. Take a firearm and signal if you find her. The rest of you check lofts, corners – anywhere a foolish child might fall asleep or hide. Catherine, you wait here in case she shows up. Sound the Newcomers' dinner bell if she does."

Catherine nodded her agreement marveling at Rebecca's propensity to wander off. *What is it with this child?* But then a frightening thought struck her. "Where's Susan?" she asked with mounting alarm scanning the area for yet another missing child, scarcely imagining they'd both disappear. "Susan!" she shouted.

"What, Mama?" Susan answered drowsily from the wagon bed where she had retreated much earlier and nearly fallen asleep.

Catherine whipped around. "Thank *Gott*. You gave me such a start, Susan. Have you seen Rebecca?"

Susan rubbed her eyes. "Not lately. I saw her carrying the snitz to the kettles hours ago, but not since." The urgency of the moment struck her. The sun was about to set and Rebecca was nowhere to be seen. The memory of the sharp scowl she had fired earlier at her now missing sister flashed through her mind. *Oh, no! It's all my fault.* She rushed to her mother's side. "Oh, Mama. I was mean to her and now she's run away." She started crying as Catherine drew her to her side. "I'm sorry, Mama. I'm so sorry. I didn't mean to. I . . ."

Catherine rubbed Susan's back as she gazed at the darkening horizon. Faint echoes of 'Rebecca' sounded from all directions. The cold and damp of the season began to descend and dispel the earlier comfort of day.

"I know, *Liebchen*. We'll find her. Pray God watches over her until then. *Lieber Gott,* please keep her safe."

-6-
The Search and Wintering- In

"Wish I could hear the creek," Rebecca said to the trees rattling above her. "Why won't you be quiet?" She hunched behind an outcropping of limestone at the far end of a recently harvested flax field to block the gusts of chill wind that had intensified over the past hour. Her modesty cape did little to stop her shivering as she studied the contours of the horizon trying to catch sight of something – anything – familiar.

Some time ago – she guessed nearly three hours – she had fled the Newcomers' farm bound for home. Not wanting anyone to see her and make her stay, she determined to take a shortcut through a small copse of woods that would hide her and get her home faster than the route the family had taken earlier. After she ducked into the brush on the far side of the clearing next to the Newcomers', she had relaxed and slowed her pace. She had hung her head and reviewed the events of this horrible day as she kicked acorns and dry leaves in front of her for more than an hour, not thinking to look around occasionally to get her bearings as her brother John had taught her.

She might still be walking aimlessly were it not for the sharp cry of a red-tailed hawk circling above that made her look up. What startled her most was not the silent swoop of the bird after a scampering rabbit, but the unfamiliar landscape. Her heart started pounding in her chest.

Recalling the time she and Susan had lost their way looking for hickory nuts, she said, "Maybe one of the tricks Oma Stoner taught us about finding our way will work again." She took a deep breath and turned around three times, "*Eins – Zwei – Drei,*" and opened her eyes. Nothing.

She closed her eyes again and took three giant steps backwards, "*Eins – Zwei – Drei,*" and looked. Still no help. Tears began to puddle in her eyes. "I only know one more. This just *has* to work." She removed her modesty cape, flipped it inside out and re-tied it over her shoulders. "*Gott im Himmel,* please show me the way," she prayed squinting her eyes tightly before once again surveying her position. But, to her despair, her prayer went unanswered.

The trees and brush that had once offered shelter and seclusion now turned dark and ominous. She made her way to the open expanse of field and wandered aimlessly until slumping in exhaustion beside the large rock where she now sat shivering, tears trailing down her cheeks.

"Rebecca!" called John. "If you can hear me, answer. It's only me – no one else."

As part of the search team at the Newcomers', John had opted to head east, toward home, having witnessed the angry glances between Susan and Rebecca that afternoon at the party. *I'm sure she just wanted to get away – not get lost. She probably tried to walk home by herself.*

"Rebecca!" He stopped briefly to listen for any sound that might help him discover her, but the whistling wind carried only the

rustling of trees. He squinted, relying more upon what he could *see* than hear, but the shadows cast in the fading sunlight by the swaying, half-clad branches and low clouds created the impression of movement everywhere he looked.

I hope this blasted wind is at least carrying my voice to her – or hers to mine.

Rebecca wiped away tears. Wedged against the rock, she wrapped her arms around her knees and watched the sun disappear below a skyline streaked with bands of magenta and orange. "I remember the sun *rising* behind us when we rode to the party today. So maybe if I walk with the sun *setting* behind me now, I'll be headed in the right direction," she reasoned. "It's better than staying here all night and freezing to death."

She pushed herself up from the cold, stubbly ground, but as she turned to head away from the setting sun, a strange shadow emerged from below the rise of the field in front of her. She ducked out of sight and froze. *What was that?* The crunching of footsteps grew louder.

Rebecca's panting quickened. *"Vater unser im Himmel . . ."* she whispered frantically.

"Rebecca!"

Rebecca paused mid-prayer. *Was that my name? Did someone call me?"*

"Rebecca!" the now clearer and more familiar voice repeated.

"John?" she whispered to herself.

"Rebecca, answer me, please."

Confirmed in her hope, Rebecca leapt up. "John! I'm over here."

As she ran to him, he bent down with open arms to receive her. She buried her face in his shoulder and he lifted her holding her tightly. As she sobbed in relief, he swayed gently to reassure her. *Just cry, Schwester,* he thought. *No need to explain now. Thank you, Lord, for keeping her safe.*

When the sobs dissolved to sniffles, he asked, "Are you ready to start back?" Her head bobbed against his chest. He stood her up beside him and took her hand. "First, to the Newcomers' to let everyone know you're fine. Then home to bed. What do you say?"

She nodded and they began to make their way back up the slight hill toward the sunset. After a few yards, she asked meekly, "Is everyone terribly angry?"

"Folks are more scared than angry right now. They'll all be glad to see you, though I suspect Papa and Mama may have *at the least* some harsh words once they know you're safe."

"Will you stay with me when we get there?"

"I'll be right here." He squeezed her hand.

She returned the squeeze and pulled their clasped hands to her cold cheek.

As they walked on in silence, Rebecca considered the welcome awaiting them. "Susan won't be so happy to see me, I think," she said fishing for John's response to her concern.

"Well, I've noticed you two are having your share of problems lately."

"She *hates* me," Rebecca blurted. "Everything I do makes her angry. And then I get so nervous and worried about upsetting her that I fumble all over myself and cause even more trouble. We used to be able to talk about everything, but lately . . ."

"Feeling like we're losing someone we care about is hard," said John. "You know, Jacob and I have been best friends forever, but things have been changing between us, too."

"Really?" Rebecca said in amazement.

"Really. Especially when talk of fighting the Redcoats and the war comes up. He and Papa see it so differently than I do. I feel as though I'm disappointing them when I can't agree with them."

"Oh, John. That's exactly the way I feel about Susan!"

"Guess we have to remind ourselves that people can disagree, but still care about one another. Life gets pretty complicated sometimes."

"Seems to me that grownups are complicated *all* the time."

John laughed. "You may be right about that. I know that the older I get, the harder my questions and problems become. It might help you to remember that about Susan. Life is two years harder for her than for you right now."

"I'll try, John, but I feel so lonely without her."

John silently considered the growing differences between him and his father. At least Jacob tried to hear him out, but not Papa. He also felt their unspoken concern because he had yet to be baptized. Their family's belief as Dunkards held firmly that this choice must be made freely, with no persuasion from others. For German Baptist Brethren, baptism marked entry into adulthood and a formal acceptance into the faith. John wrestled with this decision daily, but had not yet made his peace with it. Each day pulled him further from the family he loved. He often feared that the wall separating them would grow insurmountable – and prayed every night that it wouldn't.

"But *lonely* is not *alone*," John reminded Rebecca and himself. "God is always with us all and He has chosen us for the family we are a part of, no matter how different we may become." He stopped and knelt next to her. "We'll soon be at the Newcomers'. Listen." They could hear the faint calls of 'Rebecca' close by. "Are you ready to face them?"

Looking up at him through long lashes with pathetic puppy dog brown eyes that melted his heart, Rebecca took a deep breath and nodded bravely.

"All right then." He stood and laid his hand on her head before yelling, "We're over here. I found her." He smiled down at her and off they went. He shouted still louder, "We're over here! Rebecca's fine. She's with me."

The dark figure of one of the searchers came toward them. "Over here, men. They're over here. She's with her brother," he relayed. John recognized Abner Newcomer's voice and gave silent thanks it was not their Papa's. Herr Newcomer fired his rifle signal and the bustle of Rebecca's return began.

Daniel allowed the other guests the opportunity to leave the Newcomers' farm first. After all, his daughter was the cause of everyone's late departure and traveling after dark was best avoided.

Most of the Royer children had drifted off to sleep as they waited in the wagons.

As their turn finally arrived, Daniel paused by the bed of John's wagon. He reached into the corner where Rebecca snuggled against Susan and grabbed a firm handful of a drowsy Rebecca's hair below the base of her cap, startling her from sleep. "You should thank God that you still have your health, daughter. Remember how the Renfrew sisters lost their scalps not so far from home and not so long ago? And there were two of them doing a job for their mama – washing clothes. *You*, I believe, have *no* excuse for your behavior that I care to hear. The list of chores waiting for you tomorrow will be longer than my arm. At next Sunday Meeting, you will give your apologies and offer your services to the Newcomers and to every family who was delayed here today because of your irresponsible actions."

He released her none too gently and moved to the wagon bench beside Catherine.

No one said another word the rest of the night.

By late November, the harder tasks of harvesting and preserving the foods for the winter were nearly complete. Cabbage and salt had been crushed into the five-gallon sauerkraut crocks to ferment in the root cellar beside the dusty potatoes, orange carrots and varieties of squash packed in wooden bins of sawdust.

Cucumbers were brining or sugaring along with peaches in stoneware jars on the nearby shelves. Dried apples and cherries and full cider barrels filled the eaves of the stone house attic and summer kitchen loft. Bees had given up their honey for the season and jars of the sticky sweetness were stored away for baking.

Last week's butchering still provided fresh pork for the table and a new supply of hams, bacon and salt pork hung from the rafters curing in the smokehouse. The family gristmill had halted for the season awaiting next spring's  rye and wheat. Bulging sacks of various meals and flours would provide endless loaves of bread, baked goods, and mush for months to come. The corn husking party three weeks before had supplied more fodder for the livestock and provided dried corn for hominy and such. Molasses that had been rendered from the corncobs over blazing fires would sweeten many a winter meal.

Colder weather brought its own share of work. Mountains of firewood had to be cut, split and stacked into any available space, especially with seven hearths to keep ablaze. Dozens more candlewicks had to be dipped in hot wax and hung to dry again and again to supplement the more costly use of lamp oil on the longer dark days of fall and winter. Wool from the shorn sheep and goats and silken fibers from the flax harvest had to meet the spinning wheel, a fixture in every household. The fibers had to be made ready for the small family loom or a visit from the traveling weaver with his mammoth machine. Stone had to be quarried from local limestone beds to feed the limekiln and provide building material and whitewash. The Royers' more than 700-acre woodlot, a mile east of the farmstead, awaited winter lumbering to fuel fires, fashion fences, provide bark for the tannery and more. Buzzing would increase at the water-driven sawmill and, in any *spare* time, school in the one room log building at the edge of Waynesburg was in session.

Jacob had driven Rebecca to the homes of various neighbors for three afternoons every week for three weeks to pay her penance from apple snitzen day. Seven families had exacted their toll – patiently listening to her apology – knowing that to do otherwise would challenge Daniel Royer's edict and compromise his authority as head of the family. She had washed clothes for the Remmels and Redelspergers, dipped candles for the Fahnestocks and the Schneebergers, kneaded bread for the Kneppers, and boiled off cakes of lye soap for the Martins and the Newcomers. After evening supper, she had to fulfill the duties at home that she had missed in her absence. Susan tried to help her as best she could, but any *idle* hours were to be spent at school. While her brothers and sisters had attended as they could, Rebecca hadn't seen the schoolmaster for more than a month.

"The reading Papa selected from the Bible tonight was one of my favorites," Elizabeth shared as her fingers guided the fibers of wool onto the whirr of the spinning wheel that twisted them into a fine yarn. She stared out the window of the dining room where most of the family had remained after evening devotions.

"Yes, the parable of the lost sheep is comforting," Catherine agreed over the soft clicking of her knitting needles that were fashioning a woolen scarf. It would replace the one that had been gnarled by the gears at the gristmill when Jacob was making some repairs. Luckily he had been able to free his neck, avoiding being drawn into the machinery as well. His carelessness in neglecting to remove the scarf had been sobering. Catherine paused the rocking of her chair beside the hearth as she completed a row of stitches and held the piece at arm's length to assess her progress. "The Lord, like the good shepherd, will not abandon those who stray or lose their way. His grace is for everyone."

She glanced at John who was engrossed in the newspaper that the tinker had delivered that day. *No doubt more news of the war,* she thought reading the somber expression on his face partially blocked by an unruly shock of blond hair that had fallen as he bowed his head poring over the pages. *He's my lost sheep, that one. So troubled – so distant. Pray God soon shows him the way.*

"Fiddlesticks! My floss is all *stroubly* again," moaned Cate. She dropped the needle and tangled web into her lap.

"Let me see," said Rebecca seated beside her on the bench facing the fire. She laid her own embroidery aside and began gently teasing the loose knots from the mess in Cate's lap.

 "Before you start your sampler again, pull your needle and thread through this bunch of raw wool." She nodded toward the small, fluffy ball in her lap. "The oily lanolin will keep the floss straight."

"*Danke,*" said Cate. "You're so smart, Rebecca."

"Only as smart as Mama and Susan made me," Rebecca said catching a glimpse of Susan at the other end of the bench hemming a piece of linen for Polly's *kist*.

"And I could only teach Rebecca as much as Mama and Polly and Elizabeth taught me," Susan added.

"And someday I'll teach Nan," Cate said, brightening a bit. She looked at her sleepy little sister on the hooked rug at her feet curled into the nest of Mukki's thickening winter coat.

"And someday Rebecca and you can help fill my *kist* like I'm helping fill Polly's." Susan smoothed the finished edge of the future kitchen towel across her lap. She looked up as George Schmucker's hearty laugh and Polly's lively giggle filtered into the dining room from the parlor across the front hall. Wednesday evenings were his courting times.

"I wonder what George is *teaching* Polly right now?" Susan said. She and Rebecca grinned.

"Enough of that," Catherine softly cautioned. "Don't forget you will have prospective husbands of your own in the parlor some day."

". . . and the back yard has nearly two acres bordering on a small stand of pin oaks," George explained to Polly. "I know it wouldn't be like living in the country, but we could still have a sizeable garden of our own."

"It sounds grand, George. I'll probably take to life in Waynesburg like a bee to sunflowers." The excitement in George's hazel eyes made Polly's heart flutter in her chest. *He's wonderful,* she thought. *So strong and handsome that any girl would be thrilled to be sitting here with him. When he hugs me, I feel so safe and loved.*

"Benjamin Monn lives in the house now, but he's moving his family to Ohio to be with his wife's people after their next baby is born in May. If I keep saving my wages and building furniture after work hours, I should have enough to offer for the house by the time they leave. Uncle Cyrus isn't charging me anything for my room and board and he's ready to make me a full partner when I finish my apprenticeship in February."

"I can hardly believe it, George – *our* home. Wherever we live, it will be *our* home and I'll love it."

"Like I love you, Polly." George tussled the light-brown curls gripping the rim of her bonnet and drew his hand slowly down her smooth, rosy cheek. "I want you to be proud of me – and your papa to be glad to have me as a son-in-law." He brushed his thumb across her chin. *If you only knew how amazing you are – so alive, so loving.*

"Well, what else do you want? Because you already have those." She ruffled his tight mass of auburn curls as he had hers. "And a head of hair that out-does even mine." She grinned.

He checked the arched doorway to the hall and found no onlookers. "This," he whispered as he tilted his head and brought their lips together.

 Daniel's back office had seen few inactive days or evenings, save Sundays, since the move to the new house. The mushrooming population of Franklin County with more than 19,000 souls and the upheavals of

the war in surrounding areas – both North and South – consumed every product that the Royer farmstead had to offer. From grain to leather goods – from timber to butter – from fodder to whiskey – all had eager markets waiting.

"Lots of folks hire in the spring for planting. We'll have a better chance of getting good men if we hire now since harvest is soon over and they'll be idle," said Daniel pacing the floor as usual.

"And pockets are empty," added David from his seat in the small barrel-back chair by the fire.

"Exactly. And if the Redcoats don't soon settle down, the militias will soon have more of our workforce, too," said Daniel.

Jacob stood just inside the door still confused by the invitation to join his father and David. *Why do they want me here? And if me, why not John, too?* he wondered as he waited to be recognized. He dried his sweaty palms on the sides of his pants.

"Take a seat, Jacob," said Daniel pulling a chair away from the small table. Jacob sat, folded his hands and listened. David turned his chair to face the table and Daniel joined them. Jacob tried to imagine the possible reasons for this meeting. *Did I do something wrong? Forget something? What?*

"Jacob," Daniel began, "you did a fine job helping David manage the mill after Samuel left."

"*Danke,*" said Jacob relieved for the moment, but still dubious. *And? . . .* he thought, knowing they probably hadn't called him in here just to offer a compliment that anyone could witness.

"But the milling was already slowing down when David returned to the tannery full time and you took over the mill alone in November. This spring will be a different matter altogether," Daniel continued.

"Yes, Papa. I'll do my best," Jacob responded. *Is this a warning?* he wondered.

"I fear it'll be too much for any *one* man – maybe even *two*. You'll need help and David can't spare any tannery workers," Daniel said.

"What about John?" asked Jacob anxious to discover why his brother had been excluded from the gathering.

"That's a good question, Jacob. What *about* John?" Daniel resumed his pacing, his voice tightening. "His feelings on the war are no secret to anyone here. He might very well decide any day to pack up and join the troops. *You'll* be the one left to work with whoever we decide to hire, in addition to taking care of the farm chores that he'll have deserted. It's *you* that should have some say about who comes to work here."

David leaned back in his chair and clasped his hands behind his head. "We can find plenty of work to start at least two men next week – get the picks of the litter. Does anyone come to mind right now, Jacob?"

Jacob considered. "Well, Sean McBride has learned how to turn a good day's work since he lost his wife and baby last winter. Hasn't had a drink of whiskey since, so I hear."

"And he lives close by. That's a plus," David noted. "His younger brothers could handle the work on the few acres they lease without him."

Jacob scratched his head. "And maybe Lester Reed. His family tenant farms some acres on the other side of town. He worked harvest for the Leshers and I heard him asking last week in town if anyone was hiring."

Daniel and David nodded. But Jacob couldn't shake his concern about John's absence. He wrung his hands and felt sweat under his collar. *He'll not be pleased. It'll only push him more towards leaving. He'll really turn a deaf ear when I try to convince him that he can help the American cause as much here at home as he can by joining the fighting.* Swallowing hard, Jacob decided to risk at least a suggestion. "Maybe *John's* heard of some other prospects. I could go get him and . . ."

Before Jacob could finish, Daniel opened the door to the hall. "Go see to the livestock, Jacob. Make sure they're well stabled. By the look of this night sky, December's going to give us our first real taste of winter tomorrow."

-7-

Christmas 1813

Susan sat at the bottom of the highly polished oaken staircase in the hallway staring at the heavy front door. She was caught up in a quiet world of disbelief. *So many changes since last Christmas,* she pondered. The scent of pine seeping out of the small parlor through the arched doorway to the right drew her eyes to the family's first ever Christmas tree. The five-foot white pine decorated with garlands of popped corn, strung cookies and delicate cut paper ornaments stood in front of the frosted front window safely away from the small hearth heaped with softly glowing embers.

 *Don't know of any other Brethren family who has a Tannenbaum,* Susan thought to herself, *but George told me that Lutherans and Moravians decorate them every Christmas – and his father's a Lutheran minister.* Susan remembered her Papa's

answer when she first asked him about the tree. *'What foolishness,'* Papa had said. *'Such worldliness has no place in a house of mine!'*

Susan gazed at the soft pine branches. *But luckily Elizabeth knew what to do and say,* Susan recalled. *She waited until all of the tenants had paid their rent and then suggested to Papa that perhaps their own new house called for some new traditions.* Susan smiled. *Only Elizabeth's calm voice could have persuaded him. If anyone else had asked, Papa's 'Nein' would have woken Frau Fahnestock from a sound sleep over a mile away.*

"I remember the very words Elizabeth used," Susan whispered to Mukki, who was curled in a furry half-moon on the floor between the tree and the fireplace. "She told Papa that 'the paper star sitting atop the tree will remind us all many times each day of Jesus' birth.' How could he ever object?" She admired the creation yet again. "Of course, such a tree would have taken up nearly a quarter of the space in our old cabin."

At the sound of footfalls on the steps behind her, Susan shifted toward the beautifully turned stair spindle to make way for Rebecca who settled into the space beside her. Drawing in a deep breath, Rebecca said, "I just love the smell of warm sausages and spiced cider. It'll be a grand meal we'll be having soon." The normally substantial noon meal earlier that day had been smaller than usual in anticipation of the late afternoon holiday feast. Everyone would stuff their bellies today. The following day, Christmas, would be one of fasting and prayer.

Cate was busy placing the hammered silver spoons at each place setting around the long table in the dining room, the largest room in the house. Everything was awash in the glow of the dancing fire in the wide hearth on the far wall and the flickering candles standing among the dishes that would soon be full of hearty sauerbraten, cooked turnips, *Spätzle* with browned butter, hot cabbage slaw, steamy bacon dumplings, sauerkraut with sweet potatoes, stewed rhubarb and more. Mama, Elizabeth and Polly were adding the finishing touches at the smaller cooking hearth and iron stove in the anteroom kitchen through the door at the back of the dining room. Nan was humming softly to her rag doll as she sat cross-legged on the braided rug nearby.

 A muted thud against the stone wall beside the outside door of the dining room fireplace indicated that John and Jacob were piling up enough firewood to supply the entire household on the following day to allow more time for prayer and reflection. Daniel and David were in the back room adjacent to the parlor discussing business. The Royers' various enterprises were growing like rising yeast breads with the expanding operations of the family farmstead.

Rebecca leaned in toward Susan. "I can't wait until Sarah and Samuel get here."

"I know," Susan whispered back. "They can't stop smiling." Both girls laughed, as caught up as the newlyweds in thoughts of new love.

A knock at the front door sent the girls scrambling to be the first to welcome their favorite brother and *new* sister. Nan and Cate came flying in from the dining room and the four girls wrapped themselves around the couple in a flurry of chatter and kisses.

"Whoa!" Samuel whooped, throwing up his arms at the onslaught. "It's a pack of wild horses."

Susan and Rebecca hadn't quite gotten used to Samuel's new beard and Susan especially missed seeing his dimples when he smiled. But for Samuel, the thickening beard, a tangible sign that he was indeed a married man, was a source of great pride.

"Girls!" Mama yelled from the kitchen. "Give Samuel and Sarah room to breathe. Come help get the things to the table."

As the girls dashed to their duties – Susan to the pewter pitcher of milk and Rebecca to the bowl of applesauce – Daniel and David emerged from the hall beside the stairs. The men greeted Samuel with the kiss of brotherhood and took the couple's heavy wraps chilled by the late afternoon air.

Soon all 13 Royers were standing at their places around the table. Steam rising from the brimming dishes carried sumptuous aromas that tempted everyone's taste buds. The fire crackled in the sudden stillness as they faced each other across the table, Papa at the head and Mama at the opposite end awaiting the blessing. The parents caught each other's glance basking in the warmth of the fruits of their nearly 25 years of marriage.

Daniel clasped his hands in front of his chest and surveyed the group to ensure that all had followed suit. Everyone closed their eyes as he prayed. "*Lieber Gott*, whose love is bestowed on us in abundance each day, we give reverent thanks *für die vielen Segen* showered on our family. Although we can never be worthy of such blessings, may we strive every day to follow the example of Your son, Jesus, to whose birth we will soon pay homage. May we be humble and generous and ever mindful of your presence and of the greatest gift of all – Your precious son and the grace He grants each and every one of us.

"Bless this food that it may nourish us with the strength to do Thy will and serve Thee well. Amen."

A satisfied slump from over-full stomachs and the comfort of a flickering fire that warmed the air and spirits settled over the Royer dining table. From the blessing that began the meal to the crumbs of apple crisp and pie on the plates that signaled its end, nearly two hours had passed.

"*Mutter* Royer, your shoo fly pie was delicious. I can understand why it's one of Samuel's favorites. I hope you'll share the recipe with me," said Sarah taking her husband's hand.

"It was Oma Stoner's before me and I am pleased it will survive yet another generation. The secret's not to use too much molasses." Catherine smiled at her new daughter-in-law.

"I'm sure it will take a few tries before I can match yours, *Mutter* Royer. I'm finding the list of tasks for a farmer's wife is prodigious indeed. Growing up in town, I'm afraid I didn't properly appreciate the demands of country living." Sarah sighed.

"She's doing just fine," Samuel insisted. "Our cabin's already in fine fettle. The household came together more quickly than I expected. You won't believe the difference the next time you come to visit."

"Thank you, Husband. You're too kind," Sarah said. She turned eagerly to the other girls at the table. "But I do hope you come by soon. It's so very quiet when Samuel's out and about his work. In town, such silence and solitude is rare."

"Country living has been an adjustment for Sarah," Samuel admitted, "but . . . it won't be long until some new sounds will be disturbing the silence and blessing our home."

Sarah bowed her head and blushed.

Rebecca was the first to react leaping up from her seat on the bench. "A baby! Sarah's going to have a baby, right? . . . *Stimmt das*, Samuel?"

All eyes turned to the couple as Samuel's beaming matched the intensity of Sarah's burning cheeks. Sarah nodded. Catherine flew to her side, grasped her shoulders and kissed the top of her head as Daniel shared a pleased look of approval with his son.

In a flash, the younger girls wriggled their way in front of their Mama and began hugging Sarah's arms. David gave Samuel a firm pat on the back as brothers John and Jacob reached across the table clasping his hands in theirs. Elizabeth bowed her head in a quick prayer of thanks as Polly rushed to Sarah's rescue. Pulling the young ones back she warned, "Be careful you don't make Sarah fall right out of her seat."

"That's good advice, Polly," said Catherine herding the boisterous girls together. "Let Sarah get comfortable on the settee in the parlor before these young ones smother her with hugs."

"It's those wild horses that need corralling again," laughed Samuel.

"Now, Polly," Catherine instructed, "you help Sarah get settled in by the parlor fire and your sisters can help me *redd up* these leavings of the feast."

"Oh, I'm just fine, *Mutter* Royer. Let me help you," Sarah protested.

"Oh, you're the picture of health – especially with those rosy cheeks – but I'm declaring you the guest of honor for the rest of your visit. Your job is to join Polly in the front room and talk your hearts out about babies and weddings."

"And boys, you can all join me in the back office before the day winds down any more," added Daniel. "We have some important matters to discuss before Samuel and Sarah leave us." Only David seemed less than surprised by the request from their father, but as Daniel rose from the table they all promptly did the same and followed him out of the dining room and back the front hallway.

Honeyed vapors emanated from the fading embers of apple wood in the hearth adjacent to the small, round table in the back room that had been designated as Daniel's business office. An oil lamp still burning from the pre-dinner hours sat in the center of the table. Here the family patriarch not only worked on the necessary records of the various farmstead operations, but he also met with fellow businessmen, collected monies in his role as tax collector, and even enjoyed the occasional social meeting with friends.

He motioned to his sons to sit at the table as he stood looking out the window at the moonlight washing the dark gray rolling hills. The nearby smokehouse was one of the first structures he had built on the homestead in the nearly 35 years since Catherine's father, Abraham Stoner, had deeded the land to him. *A fine transformation, indeed,* he mused silently. Mindful of the sin of pride, he said aloud without looking at the others, "The Lord has rewarded us abundantly for our labors." He turned to them. "And with Samuel and Sarah begins the next generation that will carry on our family traditions."

"Amen," Samuel replied and his brothers echoed.

"But it's our duty to work hard with all the strength and diligence that the Lord has granted us to be worthy of such gifts." He crossed his arms over his solid chest. "In that spirit, I've been weighing some information my brother, your Uncle John, has shared with me.

"As you all know, your uncle has prospered with his iron forge operation upstate in Huntingdon County. You also know that I have shared in his financial investment and profits from Cove Forge. What you do *not* know is that he has suggested that I might invest in a similar endeavor by buying some available land near him that would be highly suitable. Such a decision is impossible without seeing the land and discussing the potential firsthand. As soon as weather permits, Samuel and I

will journey north to discover as much as we can. It's a 90-mile trip, so we'll be gone for some time."

Samuel's eyes widened at this news that affected him most directly. Daniel paused briefly to allow his sons time to process what he had just announced. "I suspect Samuel and I will be absent from home for two weeks or more. It is imperative that operations at the sawmill and tannery continue as smoothly as possible while we are gone. This war with the British has sorely stretched our ability to supply the needs of the militia and the poor souls displaced by the fighting." A knowing glance flashed between Daniel and son John at the mention of a topic so intensely debated between them.

"David will continue to oversee the tannery and business dealings. John and Jacob, it is for you to decide who will manage the sawmill and attend to household needs both here and at Samuel's. You have the new hired men to help you now, so put them to good use – make them earn their wages. Little time for leisure, even if it is winter. No planting or harvesting, but the lumbering and ice cutting from the millpond are backbreaking and require many hardy hands. I trust the three of you can handle it well."

The boys nodded at their father and then each other to confirm his pronouncement. "No problem will arise that we can't handle until your return, *Vater*," David answered.

"Sarah will prefer to stay with her family in town until I return," Samuel said, thinking of his young wife alone in their remote cabin.

"Such plans should be considered between now and our departure for Cove Forge. I thought it best to meet with you while we were all together," Daniel said. "But let tomorrow be devoted to prayers and thanksgiving for the birth of our Savior and naught else.

Nothing need be mentioned about this business until Christmas is past."

Catherine wiped her brow with the back of her hand. Despite the winter's cold blast, the compact kitchen harbored well the heat of the cooking hearth and stove. The toasty warmth coupled with the formidable cleanup tasks following such a sumptuous meal had raised quite a sweat among the girls and their mother.

Rebecca took the final clean platter from Cate and placed it on the proper shelf. "May *we* go in the parlor, now, Mama?" she pleaded.

"Better you wait here while I check with Papa about the nightly devotions. Remember how special they'll be tonight. Besides, Polly and Sarah have much to talk about that doesn't need younger ears listening. Wait here and make sure that everything's ready for tomorrow's prayer and fasting until I come for you."

"Yes, Mama," they answered obediently. Elizabeth took sleepy Nan into her lap, while Rebecca and Cate sank cross-legged in front of the fire as Susan scraped the hot coals into a mound banking them to preserve enough embers through the night to begin a fire the next morning.

In the parlor, Polly and Sarah were side by side with hands clasped so caught up in chatter about their impending momentous events that they didn't notice Catherine standing in the arched doorway. She paused for a moment before disturbing them and smiled as she recalled her own such giddiness so many years ago. *Life flies by so quickly,* she pondered. *I can scarcely believe I'll soon be an 'Oma,' but I remember so well the excitement they're feeling.* She sighed and returned to the task at hand. "Time to gather for the Bible reading, young ladies," she said.

The girls looked up at Catherine and the three were immediately caught up in a shared moment of joyous content. No one spoke, but all understood their bond and allowed themselves the time to drink it in before Polly answered, "Yes, Mama – and Mama?"

"Yes, Polly."

"I love you, Mama,"

Catherine knelt in front of them and their arms fell on each others' shoulders. "We are truly blessed by God's love and each others'," she shared.

"*Mutter* Royer," said Sarah. "I give thanks every day in my prayers that Samuel's love brought his family's love with it."

Catherine kissed both girls' hands and stood. "I'll go speak to Papa and the boys now about gathering here to share the first Christmas story – to bring us all together in our *new* home with our *new* family and give communal thanks."

Nan's deep, even breathing betrayed her lapse into sleep. The very youngest of their number was cradled in Elizabeth's arms as they sat among the dozen-plus Royers encircling Daniel in the softly lit parlor. The large, leather-bound family Bible lay open across his lap. The precious tome with its brass hinges and clasps had come across the Atlantic with his great-grandfather Sebastian in 1717 – nearly 100 years before, and had survived the voyage and depravations of the frontier to be the centerpiece of this moment. Through all the years of struggle and hardship – births and deaths – prosperity and distress, they had come to this moment together as Daniel read the passage from Luke that had been read every Christmas Eve in his memory.

"Und der Engel sprach zu ihnen . . . Do not be afraid . . . I bring you good tidings of great joy . . . Today in the city of David a Savior has been born unto you who is Christ the Lord . . .'

-8-

Threads of Change

"Just listen to that terrible pounding," Rebecca said to Susan. They were both bundled in their woolen shawls as they drew closer to the barn on their way to empty the bucket of kitchen scraps in the hog pen and feed the chickens who rarely ventured into the frigid air from their snug roosts in the henhouse.

Susan stared at the slightly ajar barn door that was leaking thump after thump from inside. Both girls flinched with every blow. "I'm surprised the cows give any milk at all with the winter cold and John attacking the dried stalks of flax that way. It certainly won't take as much sweat to comb the fibers clean with the hatchel. He's smashing them so hard with the breaker that the hulls are nearly dust when he's done." She frowned. "It's as close as he can come to battling the Redcoats, I think."

John was scarcely aware of the intensity of his rhythmic pounding as it reverberated through the barnyard. In mindless repetition, his body obeyed the dictates of the flax break – the raising and lowering of the heavy wooden beam that crushed the flax. Only such monotonous effort would release the fine filaments from inside the rough, straw-like husks. Eventually, his mother and sisters would spin the silky floss into thread to weave into the linen for the family's clothing. His upper arms ached and his eardrums vibrated from the repetition, but his mind drifted to the discussion that had taken place in school earlier in the day.

John had been the only one of all the pupils in the Bourn's Cabin schoolhouse that morning to correctly report the date of the British Army's surrender at Yorktown that marked the end of America's War for Independence . . .

"November 1781. Why, that's correct John Royer," said Francis McKeon who served as the community's part-time schoolmaster. "And can someone else tell me why 31 years later we are once again at war with Great Britain?"

A distracted silence greeted his question.

"Go ahead John, tell these dullards why," the teacher prompted.

"Because Britain is seizing American merchant sailors on the high seas forcing them into the Royal Navy and blocking our free trade. With fighting up North along the Canadian border, cutting off our harbors and the Brits riling up the Indians to our west, President Madison and Congress *had* to declare war. *That's why we have to fight.*"

"But fighting's wrong," said Galen Wingert the youngest of the Reverend Laban Wingert's sons who only moments before had been making faces at his older sister in the back row. "Papa said we Brethren aren't allowed to go to war. It's a sin to fight. Jesus tells us to turn the other cheek."

"I *know* that's what we're taught," said John. "But when another nation invades us, we just can't look the other way. We already fought one war for our freedom and now we have to fight another one to keep it."

"Wait 'til *my* Papa tells *your* Papa what you just said," Galen countered not hiding his threat.

"Well, let's leave this discussion to others more learned than we," said the teacher clearing his throat, suddenly aware that allowing this kind of free discussion might upset the very elders who were paying his salary. "Why don't you come up here with your hornbook, Susan, and show us how to make a *Sharfes* 'S.' The double-S in German looks a lot like a capital B."

John's attention returned to the present task as he put a new flax bundle into the break. *How could Schoolmaster McKeon just move onto another subject when war's so close?* he thought. *The Blue Ridge Mountains are just south of us, but with the Brits blocking the Chesapeake Bay and Philadelphia, the war's practically here. It's high time to start thinking about protecting ourselves.* He attacked the new stalks with renewed vigor.

With no apparent end to the battering, Rebecca finally asked Susan, "What should we do?"

"Wish I knew," Susan answered shaking her head. "John's been so unhappy lately. He's even having trouble asking the Lord's help since it's our religion that forbids him to fight."

"And most of the Brethren his age have been baptized by now. I know we dare not speak of it, but the silence only makes things worse." Rebecca dumped the garbage over the low, whitewashed fence into the hog trough splattered with frozen mud.

"Bam! Bam! Bam!" continued the din from the barn over the grunts and chewing of the gluttonous pigs.

"I'm afraid the best we can do is to pray for him and be as patient as we can. He smiles even less often than David these days. I miss our sweet John." Susan's shoulders slumped nearly spilling the mixture of sour grain and hay in her apron to the ground. She gathered the folds closer. "With Papa and Samuel gone to visit

Papa's brother in Huntingdon County, John has *more* chores now, but *less* chance of getting into an argument. Now you go on back to the house. No need for both of us to keep shivering when it only takes one to feed the chickens."

Winter had found the streets of Waynesburg as well as the nearby countryside.

"Careful, Sarah," Polly warned taking hold of her sister-in-law's elbow. "The puddles are icy and you're carrying a precious package. Are you sure that you're warm enough?" The bustle of Waynesburg in midday had Polly on edge. She was more cautious than Sarah who had known town living most of her life.

"I'm fine," Sarah reassured her taking a deep breath and pressing her hands against her swollen tummy. "It feels good to be outside. The fresh air makes my head and lungs feel so clean. Besides, the Monns' house is just around the corner. I'm so glad you stopped by my parents' house to visit and suggested we take a peek."

"But don't tell anyone that George is interested in buying it – not even your mama or papa. That might drive the price too high. You know how word spreads."

"Oh, I won't," Sarah promised. "I don't want you to miss the chance of living so close to where I grew up." She stopped and scanned the busy street and shops full of customers allowing a few pedestrians to pass them. "I forgot how exciting it is."

Polly noticed the longing in her eyes. "Do you miss it awfully – town life?"

"Well, I'm really enjoying being here while Samuel's away with your papa. Sometimes the peace and quiet of the country gets lonely, even when Samuel's there. But I suspect we'll have plenty of *noise* in a few months." They hugged each other and continued on, their shoes clomping in tandem on the wooden sidewalk.

As they neared the end of Mechanics Street, Polly's eyes began to glisten. She blinked to clear them and disguise her emotion from Sarah. *Why am I crying?* she asked herself. *Am I happy or scared? I wish George were here.*

"It's lovely, but not exactly the way I remembered," said Sarah as they turned the corner. "It used to be a log cabin – a lot like the one you used to live in before your family's new stone house."

"Really?" Polly looked wide-eyed at the small, two-story *brick* house with wooden shutters a few yards down the street.

"Really," Sarah said. "But I've seen this kind of change before. It costs much less to cover a perfectly fine log house with stone or brick and perhaps add a small addition than to build an entirely new one, especially if you want to stay at the same location."

Polly pictured the cabin of her childhood. *It feels so long ago – so far away.* She could say nothing over the knot in her throat. Sarah was puzzled at first, but quickly understood. She took Polly's hands and faced her. "I know how you're feeling, Polly. Change is frightening, but it's life – the seasons, falling in love, becoming a daughter *and* a mother. We keep moving forward, but we also need to look back sometimes, to keep our bearings." They looked together at the small house. "You'll miss your farm, your family – they're special and wonderful. But believe me, the new life you're starting will be wonderful, too – and special. You'll see."

The higher altitude of the arduous road to Cove Forge magnified the raw January weather.

"I'm afraid Tillie's paying the price for Sarah's good cooking," said Samuel. "This last climb has worked up a lather under my saddle. She's really puffing." Small clouds of smoky vapor rose from the mare's flaring nostrils into the winter air.

"And we've got two more steep rises before we get to McConnellsburg," Daniel warned. "Elsie's showing the strain, too. They'll really be ready for the stable tonight. With two more days of these blasted mountains and curves, they'll certainly earn their oats by the time we reach Cove Forge."

The two men halted the weary horses at the top of the ascent for a much needed breather and a look at the vast stretch of mountains and valleys. Range upon range of Blue Ridge Mountains spread out in a patchwork design of towering green trees and deforested brown swaths below them. "It takes a huge amount of charcoal to fuel these iron forges," said Daniel. "Your uncle estimates nearly an acre of lumber converted to charcoal is needed every day when they're running at full capacity. Those blast furnaces burn white-hot for hours on end to smelt the iron from the quarried ore and limestone. And once they're hot enough, the crews have to keep them going around the clock every day of the year. They *never* shut down.

"With all of the iron ore, limestone, forests and water power the Lord has given us around here, forges are cropping up alongside huge waterwheels everywhere. The Hughes brothers' operation at Mont Alto Furnace back close to home opened just six years ago. It's already an entire village – wooden shanties for all the workers, mostly Welsh and Irish. They've even got a company store, gardens and shelters for the horses, mules, pigs, chickens and cows."

"It's amazing," Samuel said. "And that ironmaster they hired and brought over from England has earned the mansion they built for him. He's figured just the right mixture of iron ore, limestone and charcoal to produce a really high quality pig iron. The process is backbreaking, but fascinating. Transforming lumps of rock into finished metal is almost magical."

Daniel shook his head. "I agree. That pig iron doesn't look like much, but think of all the hinges, nails, wheel covers and ironwork it'll make. Iron mills are the future, son. Very profitable if you can afford the investment.

"This trip should help us decide if *we* want to be a significant part of this industry. The opportunity's waiting, according to your uncle. Since he earned his ironmaster credentials and opened a modest operation at Cove Forge, he's been hungering like a spring bear to expand production. Our joint financial assets could generate a very impressive start to that end.

"If I determine to pursue this possibility, I'd need at least one of my sons to be willing to pull up stakes and move to Cove Forge to look after our family's interests." Daniel stared hard at Samuel. "A young man starting a family could make himself a fine living and full pockets at such a trade."

Samuel returned a look that said he understood full well that his father was referring to him. "I'm grateful that you invited me along. Not a minute has passed since news of my first child that I haven't wondered about how I'll provide amply for my family in the future. The acres you gifted me are fertile and much appreciated, but certainly not sufficient if my family grows to any proportion, God willing."

"Your family, large or small, will be the most important concern in your life. And, by God's grace, they'll be healthy and obedient." Daniel urged Elsie to the right, away from Samuel, as he added, "An unfaithful child is a torment to the soul."

In the heavy silence that followed this obvious reference to John, the breeze kicked up eddies of dust around the horses' shuffling hooves impatient to move on as Samuel considered his response. "I truly believe that John's a torment to himself as well, Papa. His mind has a conscience, that *unlike* ours, tells him he should fight with *every* means against those who would harm others."

"Does it also tell him to fight God? To reject the faith and tradition that his family shares?" Daniel challenged the gray sky.

"I can't speak for him, or know his heart. I can only listen and try to understand his questions," Samuel answered humbly.

Daniel pulled hard on his reins toward the road. "Enough about your brother." He nudged the horse down the slight slope toward the next challenging hill and looked over his shoulder at Samuel who followed behind. "So what do you think of the 'new' brother who'll be joining our family next harvest time – strapping George Schmucker?

"I think he's a fine man, strong as an ox and smart as a whip," said Samuel glad to move to a more congenial topic.

"I agree. I think our high-spirited Polly has met her match. Pity his father's a Lutheran pastor, but George is an upright man of good stock and their children will be formidable indeed."

Night overtook the Royer farmstead. The usual company of owls echoed the low, hollow hoots from the dark. Livestock was bedded down and David had read the evening devotions in Daniel's absence and excused his siblings to their own preoccupations.

Catherine flinched dropping her knitting to her lap at the loud crack from the dining room hearth. *The logs do that all the time. I shouldn't have jumped so,* she told herself. Mukki had not stirred and Susan and Rebecca didn't miss a stitch of their needlework. *Thank the Lord that they don't feel Daniel's absence as strongly as I do.* She peered into the dark corners of the room – imagined the even darker corners in the rooms beyond and above her. *Until now, he's been home every night since we moved. This house has grown eyes and ears after dark without him.*

Jacob hung his coat by the door having returned from the barn. David was in the back office balancing accounts and John had taken some reading to his upstairs room some time ago. Elizabeth had carried Nan to their bedroom and stayed to read her Bible by their small fireplace, while Polly took stock of the growing inventory of her *kist*. Only Susan, Rebecca and Cate shared the quivering glow of the slowly dying fire. *I pray moments like these get easier in time. I'd never wish to return to that tiny cabin, but some changes have been harder than others.*

Catherine tucked her yarn into the reed basket beside her chair. "Off to bed girls. The morning will come more quickly than you wish." *Not quickly enough for me though,* she thought. As she banked the fire to smolder until morning, she listened to the three pairs of footsteps on the stairs. "And don't forget to say your prayers," she called after them.

-9-

Winter's Arrival

*D*anke, Herr Provines," said Samuel as he tucked the woolen blanket snuggly around Sarah in the bed of the small spring wagon that Sarah's father had quickly adapted for the snow by locking the wheels with bolts and attaching wooden runners. Snowflakes had begun to accumulate in the Waynesburg area a few hours earlier as Daniel and Samuel, weary from their return trip through the mountains, made their way through Mercersburg toward home. Although the precipitation had stopped briefly, four inches of powder greeted their arrival in town.

Daniel had said his goodbyes and continued on toward the farmstead while Samuel stopped at the Provines' to collect Sarah. "The loan of your wagon sled will ease the journey home for Sarah." He smiled at his bride. *I surely missed her. These last two weeks in Cove Forge felt more like a month.* Gently squeezing her shoulder, he thought. *Hope she takes the news well.*

"No problem, Samuel." Ezra Provines gave the mare's leather cinch a firm tug and stroked her frosty mane. "Looks like Tillie's fine with the change of harness. Can't be too careful now – our firstborn *and* our first grandchild are on board. Just glad the Lord held off most of the snow 'til you and your papa got back safely."

Frau Provines secured a sturdy white oak basket of bread, hominy, bacon, and molasses cake beside Sarah and kissed the knitted scarf around her head. "You'll need the sled more for farm chores than we will here in town. Besides, it'll make visiting easier if the snow stays with us."

Samuel jumped onto the wagon bench and took the reins. The puffs of smoke from Tillie's nostrils faded into the backdrop of gray sky. Scattered flakes of large, fluffy popcorn snow started to dot the air. "Looks like the storm's waking up again. Best be going while the light's still good. The days are so short now." He looked at Sarah. "Are you ready, Wife?"

Sarah's blush of affection glowed in contrast to the otherwise drab scene. "I am, Husband."

Tillie pulled away kicking up small drifts of snow as her passengers waved their goodbyes to the Provines' household gathered on the front porch. "Godspeed," called *Frau* Provines. She took her husband's arm.

"Godspeed, indeed," he repeated gently patting her hand.

Daniel Royer took stock of his blanketed farmstead as he rode Elsie directly to the barn. Smoke poured from all the chimneys of the stone house. *Gut,* he noted. Looking down, he felt further reassured by the runner tracks in the new snow. *Wagon has its sled runners.*

"Looks like all's well so far," he told the weary horse as he dragged the saddle and tack to their wall pegs. After smoothing her matted coat with a few well-deserved strokes of the stiff grooming brush, Daniel dumped some oats in her feed trough and broke the ice on the water bucket beside it. "*Gute Arbeit,* Elsie. Rest well."

As he made his way toward the house, he noticed the slender, gracefully curved runners of the family sleigh as it stood in the far corner of the barn. He glanced up to the high rafters where it hung most of the year and smiled. "Looks like someone will be wanting a sleigh ride soon."

He pulled the barn doors closed behind him, paused and squinted to bring into focus the not-too-distant road that adjoined the entrance to the farmstead. *Samuel and Sarah should be coming by soon. Be good to know they're safely on their way.* All was still and silent in the tableau before him, but he lingered. Then he caught sight of some movement in the distance and squinted harder. "Ah, there they come." He cupped his leather-gloved hands around his mouth and shouted, "Samuel! Sarah!"

The dark spot on the road slowed. "Yes, Papa," came the hollow echo in response.

"*Gute Nacht*!" Daniel yelled toward Samuel's arms waving high above his head.

"*Ja, gute Nacht*," came a second greeting from the open front door of the stone house. Catherine stood on the front porch waving her arms just like her son.

"*Schlaf gut,* Mama!" Samuel's distant voice added as the wagon sleigh faded into the dusk.

Daniel and Catherine stared serenely at each other across the expanse of the barnyard. As she waited hugging her shawl around her shoulders, he ploughed his way toward the house. "Hello, Catherine," he said as he stepped up to greet her grasping her shivering arms and kissing her forehead softly. "All is well?"

"It is now," she whispered.

By sunrise more than eight inches of fluffy down clung to every niche of the countryside – so much white that the shadows cast by trees and buildings shone icy blue. Translucent gauze wound around broad tree trunks. Delicate, white snakes lay evenly atop a glistening spider web of bare branches and mounds of meringue pressed the broad boughs of the firs to the ground. The creek bit jagged edges from the frozen banks and the thickening, clouded ice muffled the burbling currents beneath. A skim of clouds muted the slate sky softening the otherwise blinding reflection of the new day's sun.

Cate's warm breath fogged a halo on the chilled panes of the dining room window as she gazed spellbound at the wonder. Her trance softened when she spied Mukki trotting out from behind the blanketed smokehouse matching her bounding steps to the faint tracks left behind by a white-tail deer in the pre-dawn hours. "Oh, Mama," she squealed. "It's like sitting on a cloud. Do you think heaven looks like this?"

Catherine gathered the bowls crusted with traces of corn mush and molasses from the table. "I'm sure heaven's beautiful, but we're still on earth with work to be done. The menfolk are already going about their business. Now help me finish clearing the table, *schnell*. And fetch the kraut and turnips from the cellar. When the sleigh pulls away later this afternoon, it'll leave behind a clean house with no chores left undone. Work before play – *Arbeit macht das Leben süß*. So if you want life to be sweet, get to work – *zur Arbeit gehen*." Catherine tried not-too-successfully to sound stern when pitted against the beckoning power of the season's first significant snowfall. With her husband and son safely home, she, too, couldn't help but surrender to the peaceful magic of the moment.

"Upstairs hearths are swept and set for tonight," Susan announced entering from the front hall carrying a tin bucket full of ashes. She pulled a woolen shawl from the row of wooden pegs by the back door and exited to dump the contents into the ash barrel just outside. By spring the discarded ash would leach into the lye they needed to mix with excess cooking fat to make soap.

Elizabeth was stationed at the kneading board of the dough tray in the winter kitchen softly humming as she pummeled the large, yeasty ball over and over with her floury hands. Nan sat on the rug next to her playing with her own small bit of dough. "There's no such thing as work on a day like today," Elizabeth said to the winter scene on the other side of the window. She pulled at the dough to divide it into six loaves for the second raising by the warm, five-plate iron stove.

"Speak for yourself, *Schwester*," Polly grumbled as her large paring knife clacked against the small work table where she quartered onions to add to the venison stew for the noon meal. She wiped the tears dripping down her cheeks with her shoulders. "The longer these onions are in the cellar, the more *scheußlich* they get." She looked up at the rafters to avoid the vapors. "I can't wait to feel the cold air in my eyes when we go sleighing. It can't come too soon."

Rebecca backed into the kitchen from the cellar pushing the heavy oak door open with her backside. Her left hand gripped the hem of her apron laden with turnips and her right hand was hooked around the lip of a two-quart crock of sauerkraut. "At least the smell of the sauerkraut only hurts noses," she said noting Polly's red eyes.

Cate rounded the corner from the front hall into the dining room. A towering pile of blankets rested in her outstretched arms. She peeked around her burden to avoid a collision as she made her way to the wooden bench by the door where she dropped them in a heap. "Will this be enough for the sleigh?"

Catherine crossed her arms over her chest and laughed. "Enough for at least *three* sleighs, I'd say. You need to leave room for the riders."

"And the foot warmers," Susan reminded her having caught the end of the conversation as she returned from her errand with an empty bucket.

Nan leaned against Susan's skirt tossing her dough ball back and forth in her small hands. Catherine took note of the action and said, "Elizabeth, start up a second batch of dough. No doubt Polly, John and Jacob will be thinking of a sledding party soon and that means pretzels for eats. Might as well take this first batch and bake them today while the oven's fired up and we're wintered-in."

"*Ja*, Mama," said Elizabeth. "Pretzels are almost as much fun to make as they are to eat."

She rolled a ball of the dough back and forth on the floured board with the palms of her hands until it formed a long rope and then separated it into one-foot lengths. Taking one piece at a time, she made a loop crossing the ends and then pressed them into the outer edge. For her, pretzel making was a prayerful reverie. The ends of the twisted dough on the upper edges of the pretzel looked like arms folded across the chest with the palms resting on the shoulders – the way medieval monks would pray. And the three openings represented the Trinity. She looked at the first of many she would shape for the oven and thought, *Three holes – one each for the Father, Son and Holy Ghost, held fast by praying hands.*

"Vater, Sohn und Heilger Geist," Elizabeth murmured as she pressed the shape into the sprinkling of coarse salt nearby and gently placed it on the baking pan, trusting that the tasty treats would remind everyone who ate them to pray.

Polly, lost in her thoughts of George trudging through the cold with the other men, smiled through her onion tears imagining his return and the happy gathering to come. "You're right, Mama. The roads should have a good, tight pack by Saturday."

"Susan, set a pot of cider on the stove, Catherine said. "The men will be half-frozen when they get back here. They've been up by the light of the moon dragging paths to the outbuildings and *Holzhaufen* before the snow cover gets ahead of them and puts too much strain on Siggy. She's done a lion's share of work, even for such a hardy mule."

"Oh, Mama, the woodlot's nearly two miles away. Will they be too tired to sleigh when they get back?"

"Well, I can't make any promises, but Papa had Jacob stay behind to handle the livestock – *and* to hitch up the sleigh and grease up the runners."

Samuel's wide-brimmed hat and worn, canvas coat hung inside the door above the wet boots that puddled on the packed-dirt floor of the small cabin. The cider in his tankard had cooled enough for him to sip some warmth into his stomach. He set the cup on the floor, leaned back in the larger of the two ladder-back chairs gifted to him and Sarah by her family, and stretched his damp woolen socks toward the blazing hearth.

Steam rose from the bubbling cast-iron Dutch oven tucked at the base of the hot embers. The hearty chicken corn soup dotted by fluffy rivel dough balls made him eager for the noon meal, but not as hungry as he was for Sarah to say something – anything – about last evening's conversation. He stared at the fire listening to her arrange plates on the table and slice the bread her mother had sent along with them in the wagon sled. *'Gott im Himmel,' let her be at peace with it. I know things have been changing so fast but* – he recalled the old German saying – *'Die Qual der Wahl.'* Now he knew firsthand 'the torture of choosing.'

Sarah moved into the halo of the fireplace, lowered herself into the chair beside Samuel and took his hand. *"Alles ist gut, mein Liebling,"* she whispered. She knew she need say no more.

Samuel sat up and leaned toward her taking her other hand. *"Ja, mein Engel. A*s long as we're together, *alles ist sehr gut."*

"How soon do we need to leave our new home?" she asked. "I know it sounds so *dumm*, but, as much as I missed town life, I'll miss *unser kleines Haus,* too."

He looked around the whitewashed walls and freshly hewn rafters. *"Ein kräftiges Haus.* I built it strong – to last as long as our love." He tilted his head and kissed her. "If we put in the first spring plantings, Papa says we should have no trouble leasing it to good tenants in April on Signing Day. Then," he said laying his hand on her stomach, "if your family will have us, we can stay with them until the baby's born."

 She put her hands on top of his and returned the kiss. "I'm sure they'll let us stay with them. And it'll be a comfort to have Mama with me when my time comes."

Energized by the confirmation of the new possibilities opening to them, Samuel moved to the window. Focusing on the far, frozen horizon he began to pour out his vision of their future. "I intend to ask Mr. Overmyer for work at that new forge he's overseeing that started just a few miles north of here. It's part of the Hughes' operation at Mont Alto Furnace and should give me a good start on my ironmaster apprenticeship until we leave for Cove Forge.

"You should see Mont Alto Furnace, Sarah. Never seen so many men working together in one place. With the wages from my new job and the lease payments on the cabin, we'll be able to offer your parents something for their hospitality *and* save for *unser neues Haus*." He turned to her. "Once in Cove Forge, we can stay with my Uncle John for a time. He's a gentle soul. You'll love him, Sarah."

Rebecca burrowed beside Susan into the featherbed made toasty by the long-poled brass bed warmer they had passed between the layers of bedding minutes before. The heated brick inside transformed the ice-cold bedding into a cozy nest. She pressed her open palms against her face. "I can still feel the cold air on my cheeks. *Es war wunderschön* riding in the sleigh today – like being wrapped in a gigantic, cold cotton ball." She giggled and propped her head on her hand. "After chores tomorrow, maybe we can find the old shovel heads and ride them down the hill from the gristmill. I'm sure Schoolmaster McKeon won't be having school."

"I doubt we'll be going to classes before next week," Susan agreed, but she was thinking more about the upcoming young peoples' sledding party than gliding down the hill with the youngsters. "We'll just have to wait and see." She rolled over and closed her eyes.

Rebecca pressed closer and whispered in her ear, "But what if . . .?"

Susan squeezed her eyes tight. "Rebecca?"

"What?" Rebecca stammered.

"You know what else was *sehr schön* about the sleigh ride today?"

"What?"

"The *quiet*!"

Rebecca frowned and swallowed the rest of her comments. Her head sank into the cool feather pillow and she was soon lost in the glowing reds and oranges wavering in the bedroom fireplace. The flickering light, along with Cate's soft, measured breathing coming from the sleeping pallet against the far wall, finally made Rebecca's eyes too heavy for her to resist sleep.

-10-

Handling the Hardships

After evening devotions with the early darkness and frigid grip of February, most of the family who were gathered around the parlor hearth would hurry to the warmth of their beds. Despite the layers of linsey-woolsey and bulky knitted sweaters and shawls, Catherine and the children shivered and their teeth nearly chattered. But this evening something was more chilling than the air. Daniel Royer's normally resonant voice had turned to harsh gravel as he began reading the passage from Psalms 46. Sweat glistened on his brow and the ashen pallor of his drawn cheeks was evidence that the family's formidable patriarch was under siege.

Daniel had abandoned his usual erect posture and sat stoop-shouldered over the family Bible. *"God is our refuge and strength, A very present help in trouble . . ."* He drew a deep, labored breath. *"Therefore, we will not fear, though the earth . . .* cough, cough *. . . though the earth be removed, and . . .* cough,

cough, cough . . . *and though* . . . cough, cough, cough." Daniel turned from the group and buried his mouth in his handkerchief. The hacking cough escalated to a strangled gagging before it finally ceased.

The awful irony of the Biblical passage he had chosen was obvious to all but the youngest present. No one had moved as Daniel struggled, knowing their father's aversion to what he would perceive as pity rather than concern if they were to offer help. When he regained his breath and faced them again, his forbidding expression left no doubt they were to remain still and silent.

With a hesitant and sorely strained voice he said, "David will finish the reading and . . ." He wheezed struggling for a breath. ". . . and Mama will offer the prayer." He passed the heavy Bible feebly to David seated beside him. David grabbed it and searched for the passage his father had been reading as Daniel drew his body against the back of his chair and closed his eyes, listening.

". . . *though the earth be removed and though the mountains be carried into the midst of the sea . . .* ," David continued solemnly.

" . . . Amen," said Catherine.

"Amen," echoed the children along with a hoarse 'Amen' from their Papa.

Daniel stood and paused to gain his bearings before crossing to the front hall where he took a firm grip on the stair railing to support the torturous climb to his bedroom. The parlor was as silent as a tomb until he was clearly out of earshot.

All eyes were on Catherine – even David deferred to her authority in this. She paused a long moment, staring at her work-worn hands folded in the lap of her apron to collect her thoughts. They waited anxiously until she finally raised her head. With a stolid strength of purpose, she surveyed her children. *Surly David, serene Elizabeth, stubborn John – more like his father than either of them knows – sweet Jacob, wise Susan, busy Rebecca and my moppets, Cate and Nan.* Without faltering she turned to her eldest. "David, you will go to town at dawn and bring Dr. Bonebreak to Papa . . . and don't come back without him."

He nodded.

"John and Jacob," she continued. "Gather your hunting gear tonight. I need fresh meat to make Oma Stoner's healing broth. Tonight's snowfall should help you track tomorrow."

The boys looked at each other. "Yes, Mama."

"Polly – Susan – Rebecca." She held the eyes of each of them in order. "You work together to keep the kitchen and carry out farm chores as usual. I'll help as I can, but I must think of Papa first.

"Cate and Nan." They ran to Catherine's open arms and clung to her skirts as she embraced them. "Now, mind your older sisters and be as quiet as snowflakes while we take care of your Papa.

"Elizabeth, I sense that he'll abide only you or me at his side. Too much concern – the presence of those who depend on the strength he has lost – will only feed the illness he's battling. The rest of you, as all of us, will serve him best with our prayers." She rose to signal their adjournment and attention to the tasks as assigned. "Now, off to bed as soon as you can.

"Elizabeth, take a lantern to the attic and gather some hyssop and Holland root for a poultice. Polly, fetch some horseradish from the cellar. We need to mix some of that in, too. Bring everything to me in the kitchen while I dampen some compresses and steep some sassafras tea. We've a long night ahead."

Jacob tapped lightly on the side of the powder horn to funnel some fine gunpowder into the muzzle end of his Papa's Pennsylvania rifle.

"*Gut,*" said John. "Now press the ball onto one of the cloth patches from the pouch and use the rod to push them down the barrel until they reach the powder."

Jacob followed the instructions intently, keeping a firm grip on the weapon as he glanced sideways over the stock of the rifle at his brother, anxious for approval. Being entrusted with their father's prized rifle – one so artfully crafted and signed by Waynesburg's very own gunsmith J.H. Johnston – was a rare privilege for a 14-year-old. John himself had only fired it a handful of times at New Year's Day shooting matches, but as the older brother, John was now passing this knowledge to Jacob. This was no holiday shooting competition. The necessity of the moment meant that he must be able to load the rifle on tomorrow's hunting trip. Their father's life might well depend on their success.

"Sehr gut," John said. "Come morning when we get closer to some wild game, we'll put a bit of powder in the pan, and then sparks will fly! We'll get a rabbit or two. You'll see." He pointed to a small compartment between the barrel and the wooden stock where a flint would ignite the charge once the trigger was drawn and pulled. This simple action transferred a spark to the main powder in the barrel. The resulting explosion would send the lead ball hurtling toward the target and put one unlucky rabbit closer to the kettle.

Jacob imagined the deep breath he would take right before he pulled the trigger and experienced the loud crack, acrid smoke and recoil of the barrel stock against his shoulder.

John took the rifle from Jacob. He admired its easy balance despite the length of the barrel and the weight of the iron. His fingertips brushed over Johnston's etched signature on the silver firebox and felt the smooth surface of the finely polished metal and sanded walnut stock. He stood it securely by the back door and carefully hung the powder horn and patch bag on the wall hook.

He patted Jacob soundly on the back. "You did a fine job and it'll get easier every time you fire it. Now we need to get some sleep so we're strong and sharp for tomorrow morning."

"Danke, Bruder. Hope I can aim as well as you teach."

"Tomorrow will tell," John said. "Let's both do our best now to rest well." As they made their way up the front stairs to their room, the grandfather clock in the hall chimed the hours.

Susan and Rebecca lay next to each other on their backs gripping the edge of the featherbed under their chins and staring at the blank ceiling. They were too distraught to sleep – afraid to close their eyes because of what the morning might bring.

"Everything has been going so well – our beautiful new house, Samuel and Sarah's baby," Rebecca said to Susan. "Except for Schoolmaster McKeon's sour face at school and the cold weather, we've not had a care in the world. Even John's been smiling more since the sledding party when he stole *einen Kuß* from Ruthie Knepper. But now . . . I'm frightened, Susan. What would we do without Papa? I know he's terrible strict, but I feel safe with him protecting our family."

"Papa will be *fine*; you'll see," Susan said flatly trying to convince herself as much as Rebecca. "He'll be bellowing at us for spilling the milk or dropping an egg again before long. And don't say 'without Papa' anymore – not out loud. We *have* to believe that God will watch over him – and us." *Or help us to continue without him,* she added silently, tears welling in her eyes.

She rolled to her side with her back to Rebecca. *Dear God, please don't take our Papa from us. I have mean thoughts sometimes when he gets so angry, but I know that he demands our obedience to keep us safe. Please, God, watch over our Papa like he watches over us. Give him strength to fight this sickness and I'll try harder to be loving and obedient.* She wiped her wet cheek on her pillow.

A flood of wrenching coughs and gagging soaked through the closed door of their parents' bedroom and echoed around the upstairs hall into the other bedrooms. Only the two youngest would find sleep tonight.

"Bam!" The report of the Royer's Pennsylvania rifle reverberated in the crisp morning air of the stark, ice-crusted valley.

"*Ausgezeichnet!*" cheered Jacob as the second rabbit that morning bloodied the snow.

"Good shot. That's one for each of us, *Bruder*." John slipped his hunting blade from his waistband. "Let's dress them both so Mama can get started on the broth as soon as we get home. The hawks will be grateful for the scraps."

After he tucked the first skinned rabbit in his larger leather pouch, John passed the knife to Jacob. "You take care of the other one. My hands are frozen," he said cupping bluish hands around his lips and blowing warm air to revive them.

"It was the ice harvesting that did it," John muttered to himself as Jacob split open the animal's chest cracking its delicate rib cage.

"What?" asked Jacob unable to make out his brother's last words.

"The ice harvest at the millpond last week. Remember when Papa gave Laban Wingert his scarf to replace the one he'd lost?" John asked. Jacob nodded. "Well," John continued, "later that morning Papa worked up quite a sweat stacking blocks in the ice house and I saw him shaking like a fall leaf when he rode the sled back up for the next load. That's when the sickness got him."

"I can't remember Papa ever being sick before. Can you?"

"Never."

The silence that followed voiced the concerns neither one would speak aloud, the disbelief that their father could be vulnerable to anything – and the fear they kept hidden.

Tossing the second pile of steaming entrails aside, Jacob held up both carcasses. "*Gottes Willen*, this meat will give him strength."

"*Du hast Recht!*" John said. "No time to waste. *Wir müssen schnell gehen!*" They gathered up the rifle and their offering and ran as quickly as the snowpack would allow toward home.

"Look! There's Doc Bonebreak's horse." John pointed ahead as he and Jacob trudged the final hundred yards to the rear of their house. Mukki sprang from her post at the back door when she spied the boys and fairly flew past the sleeping four-square garden and across the field to greet them.

"Hey, girl," said Jacob holding their recent kill at an arm's length. "Look what we've got for Papa." The dog stretched her snout toward the offering and sniffed her approval.

The group pushed in through the kitchen door and the boys shed their coats and hats. John stood the rifle with great care in the corner as Jacob presented the rabbits to Polly.

"*Sehr gut*," Polly said. "I'll start the pot boiling while . . ."

"I'll go tell Mama we've got meat for the broth," said Jacob heading for the dining room.

"I don't think that . . . ," Polly began. But he was on his way up the front stairs before Polly could suggest that he wait until Dr. Bonebreak left.

Heavy drapes in the front bedroom blocked the noon sun that might disturb Daniel's fitful rest. The small hearth barely contained a blazing fire that intensified the scent of pungent healing herbs that saturated the heavy air. As Dr. Bonebreak leaned over far enough to lay his ear against Daniel's chest, his grizzled beard rose and fell with Daniel's labored breathing.

The black leather medical bag containing various vials and instruments gaped open on the floor beside him. Dr. Bonebreak lifted Daniel's drooping eyelids and studied the glassy, bloodshot

 stare. A damp compress lay across the fevered brow. Then he sat back and cradled Daniel's wrist in his hand pressing his thumb against a vein as he flipped open his pocket watch to measure the pulse. Next to the oil lamp on the bedside table sat a thick glass jar of water alive with dark vines and black, slimy crescents.

Jacob, having developed second thoughts about intruding, slowed his pace as he approached his parents' bedroom in the upstairs hall. *I know Mama will be happy to hear about the rabbits, but perhaps not so happy to have me in the sickroom with Papa.* The door was slightly ajar, so he paused to listen before deciding if he should go in. Unable to hear clearly what was being said, he dared to move closer and look inside.

Jacob saw Dr. Bonebreak seated next to Daniel. The doctor clicked his pocket watch closed and looked at Catherine standing at the foot of the bed. "The deep rattle I hear isn't healthy, but it's a good sign that the contagion hasn't taken a firm hold. Nothing more to be done but wait and pray."

Jacob was able to catch some of the conversation. He struggled to see his father's face.

Ach, mein Gott! He barely controlled the gasp that would have revealed his presence when he spied a squiggling black cluster just below Daniel's chin. *Leeches! I hate those disgusting creatures,* thought Jacob shuddering as he watched Dr. Bonebreak pinch the heads of the parasites one by one to release their hold on Daniel's sallow skin. Using wooden tongs, the doctor returned the squirming, engorged creatures to the jar. Daniel's skin was a rash of red pockmarks where the leeches had been feeding only moments before.

"We can only hope my ugly helpers have sucked enough of the infection from Daniel's throat to help him breathe more easily," the doctor told Catherine. As he closed his bag and stood, he moved to her side and laid a reassuring hand on her shoulder. "Daniel's one of the strongest men I know – in body *and* spirit. And you are attentive nurses. *Mit Gottes Gnaden,* he'll come around. The next two days will tell."

Elizabeth had her back against the bedroom wall just inside the door staying clear as the doctor attended to Daniel. Through the doorway Jacob was able to see her clearly, although she was unaware of him. Her hands rested softly against her chest. Her head was gently bowed, but she still kept a watch over her father. Her powerful, deep calm struck him.

Jacob shook off his wonder and started to enter the room. He stopped short as Daniel suddenly began to writhe and moan as he thrashed his head back and forth on his dampened pillow. Elizabeth swept to her father's side and knelt taking hold of his flailing hand and pressing his palm against her cheek. As the others watched, she bowed her head and prayed, *"Der Herr ist mein Hirte . . .* I shall not want. He maketh me to lie down in green pastures . . . *"*

Daniel's movements began to calm. His breathing eased and his body drooped into a heavy sleep. A transcendent glow enveloped the room as a solemn reverence stilled everything around them until Elizabeth gently rose and settled into the rocker next to the bed stand.

Jacob was unable to move – frozen by a sudden awareness of the intense power of his sister's spirituality. *God is truly in her – and now with Papa.* Of this, Jacob was absolutely sure. To disturb such a moment was unthinkable. He backed away and sat at the top of the stairs to collect his thoughts. News of the hunt would reach his mother soon enough. For now, the radiant faith he had just witnessed was warming his soul.

The dining room table was spread for the noon meal. Susan had laid an extra plate for the doctor, but he declined the tempting invitation hoping to visit yet one more homebound patient before stopping to eat.

"*Danke, Herr Doktor*, said Catherine. We're grateful you ventured out on such a cold day." The doctor wound his woolen scarf around the upturned collar of his coat. Catherine handed him some freshly baked apple muffins tied in a homespun napkin. "For you and *Frau* Bonebreak and your young ones."

Dr. Bonebreak tucked the bundle into his coat confident that several coins as payment for his services rested alongside the food. It wasn't fitting to discuss such financial matters in this hour of need. "*Vielen Dank, Frau* Royer. If Daniel worsens, send one of your boys for me again. Waynesburg is not so far as to keep me from coming. *Möge Gott Sie segnen.*"

"May God bless you, too," said Catherine shutting the door against the crystalline cold.

Three tedious days had come and gone. The emotional tension and claustrophobia of prolonged close quarters played on everyone's nerves. The recent siege of intense wind and sleet had denied them even the respite of school. Although Daniel's nightly coughing fits had lessened, his absence from the family circle was still sorely felt and fed everyone's irritation and impatience.

The girls gathered around the dining room table with parchment and tiny scissors after Catherine had reminded them that

Valentine's Day would find them with no tokens of affection to share if they didn't get busy with their *Scherenschnitte*. Polly gently smoothed the ridges from the completed four-heart pattern she would give to George thinking, *Last year I had to hide the valentine I made for him. This year our love is no secret. This time next year I'll be his wife.*

Catherine had hoped her daughters' concentration on the delicate creations of intricately folded and cut paper would distract and calm them and offer a welcome break from additional afternoon chores. Even Cate was making a valiant attempt at a string of four paper dolls holding hands. But peace was not to prevail.

"*Verflucht*," spit Rebecca. She slapped her scissors on the table, crumpled her latest attempt and flung it past Polly's nose into the fire.

"Stop wasting the parchment!" snapped Susan appalled by the outburst.

"Stop telling me what to do!" Rebecca fired back. As she reached across the table for a new sheet, she bumped Susan's cutting hand. A large corner of the folded parchment Susan was working on for her Oma Stoner dropped to the floor.

"*Dummkopf!*" Susan yelled.

John laid aside the broadsheet he was reading with more news of the war, Jacob looked up from his progress stitching a frayed leather harness, and Nan dropped her corn husk doll beside Mukki who lifted her head from the warm hearthstones and barked.

All eyes were on the battling girls. No one was aware of the newest presence in the conflict-charged room.

"Silence!" roared a fearful, but familiar voice.

After a collective jump, all heads turned to the front hall archway. The sight of Papa, arms crossed over his expanded chest, his eyes flashing with renewed vigor, left everyone momentarily speechless.

Catherine stood in the far corner laughing so heartily at the flustered reaction of her children that even Daniel couldn't sustain his stern expression. "Well, Husband," she said finally. "That was an entrance none of us will soon forget." Tears of joy welled in her eyes as each child in turn welcomed their father's return to the hearth. Each embrace was the answer to many, many prayers.

Daniel moved to his wife's side. "It will be a joyful devotion of thanksgiving tonight. *Gott ist wirklich sehr gut.*"

-11-

The Spring Thaw

Susan sloughed through the mire of the freshly thawed path from the smokehouse to the summer kitchen. The weight of the rasher of bacon slung over her back counterbalanced her efforts to hold her new, longer skirts above the sticky dark mud. Along with her eleventh birthday had come ankle-length hemlines, more modest than the shorter styles of younger girls and harder to keep clean. "Thank Goodness Polly's George helped John to lay those fieldstone walkways from the house to the summer kitchen and privy last fall. As many times as I visit those two places, I wouldn't see clean shoe leather until Easter if those paths were as mucky as this."

Beads of sweat trickled down the inside of her bodice by the time she reached the threshold of the summer kitchen. The top half of the split Dutch door was open wide to help ventilate the fumes of the mixture of lye and fat bubbling in the huge cast-iron kettle suspended over the hearth.

"Phew!" Susan wrinkled her nose as she peeked in at Rebecca stirring the mixture with a large wooden paddle. Rebecca's eyes were tightly shut and her neck was twisted as far away as she could manage from the billowing steam that had plastered a fringe of black ringlets in a circle framing her face. *Maybe dirty shoes aren't so bad after all,* thought Susan.

"My eyes couldn't stand this soap making more than twice a year," Rebecca sputtered when she spied her sister.

Susan pushed through the lower half of the split door and heaved the slab of bacon onto a hook on a rafter above the iron stove laden with simmering pots for the noon meal. "It's a nasty job, but we'll need more soap than ever for spring housecleaning this year. Last year our *whole house* was just a little larger than this summer kitchen. But, you know Mama. Next month she'll want to turn the big *new* house inside out and scrub it clean of winter from ceiling to floor."

As she got closer, Susan noticed the red rims of Rebecca's eyes. She heard the hollow popping of thick bubbles as they burst and splattered on the surface of the liquid. "Here, let me have a turn with the paddle," Susan offered. "I've had enough fresh air for now. I can thaw my feet and cheeks while you spread the table for the tannery workers. When I hung the bacon by the stove, I could smell the hog maws stewing in the roaster on the two back plates."

"Thanks," said Rebecca passing the stir stick to Susan and rubbing her eyes fiercely with the backs of her hands. "We'll all eat well soon. Polly came in more than an hour ago and fed the bake oven some pumpernickel, biscuits and two big tins of apple pandowdy."

"David will be the only man at our family noon dining table," Susan reported. "The rest have gone north to set the spiles in the maples. Won't be long until the buckets are brimming with enough sap to have a sugaring off. Next hard freeze, they'll haul the big pot out to the woods and hang it from the cross timber between the two big oak trees near the clearing."

"Oh, Schwester. Remember when they went to set the spiles last year? It sends a chill through me every time I think about it." Rebecca imitated a shivering as she took a stack of tin plates from the shelf above the work sink.

"How could I forget? Since that day, my arm starts throbbing where I broke it every time I pass the lime kiln. With the rest of the menfolk away in the woods that day, if it hadn't been for George . . ."

Polly arrived with an empty basket looped over her arm and a pitcher of cider in hand just in time to catch the last of the conversation. "If it hadn't been for George," she repeated as she interrupted, "saving the two of you from the frozen creek by the kiln that day, I might be minus two sisters *and* a betrothed." She smiled and set the jug in the middle of the large plank table. "As it turned out, I thank God every day for sparing your lives and letting Papa come to see George as a fitting husband for me. Our Lord certainly works in mysterious ways."

Then she inspected the progress of the soap kettle. "Looks like you can swing that away from the fire, Susan. Let's get rid of some of the stink before it's time to eat. We can scoop most of it into crocks for smear soap when it cools. Then we can cook the rest a little longer for hard cakes."

"We'll want to *keep* the sweet smell in here on *Fastnacht Day*. What a grand place this will be for making all of those delicious doughnuts before Lent!" said Susan.

"And then we'll use the leftover grease to oil the tools for waking up the four-square garden. I can hardly believe spring is really that close," said Rebecca.

"But not as close as noon meal," Polly reminded them. "If you want time to eat without swallowing your food whole, best step up your pace. Cate's nearly finished with her setup chores in the dining room. Before you blink it'll be time to ring the dinner bell for the workers.

"*Ja*," said Susan. "Rebecca and I will fetch the soap crocks down from the loft in here and finish up this chore *in keiner Zeit*."

Polly moved to the bake oven next to the hearth and opened the cast-iron doors. Wavering currents of heat heavy with the aroma of fresh bread and simmering apples escaped. She slid the long-handled wooden spatula in and under the loaves and baking tins one by one and tipped them onto the work table to cool. She shut the oven door.

"Ouch!" she cried licking her singed fingertips after transferring most of the hot bread into her basket. "You two bring one of the maws and a pandowdy to the house with you. I'll tell Mama you're on your way." As she pushed outside through the door, she paused to study the horizon. "Gray clouds are rolling in. I sure hope the men get the maples tapped before it ices up again. Sugaring off can't come too soon for me."

The column of steam rising from the boiling maple sap in the immense black kettle carved a dark halo into the snow-capped branches directly above it. A second circle of pockmarks dotted the soft snow below as the trees just outside of the halo's radius dripped their white coating to the ground. Daniel kept close watch at the intense fire continually skimming the froth from the surface of the liquid with a long-handled ladle to prevent the kettle from boiling over.

Cate, Rebecca, and Susan sat nearby on the low, oak sled used to haul the heavy equipment to the clearing nearly a mile from their house. Samuel pressed ten empty cedar buckets into the snow to steady them. They were sticky with a coating of the sap that had drained into them from the tapped maples. Susan looked over at him and sighed. *This is Samuel's last maple sugaring with us. It just won't be the same without him. Cove Forge is 'so weit weg' – so far away indeed.*

The three children each held a small tin saucer in their lap anxiously waiting for word from Papa that the sap was ready. This was one time Susan enjoyed being counted as 'a child.' When enough water had cooked away, the liquid would begin to thicken into syrup.

Jacob came out of the edge of the woods into the clearing yoked like a mule with a curved wooden crossbar over his shoulders that had buckets full of fresh sap suspended from ropes at  each end – the last of the gatherings. A small ladder was propped against one of the two trees that cradled a strong cross timber that held the chain suspending the kettle over the fire. When he reached the base of the ladder, Jacob bent at the knees until the buckets sat on the ground. Polly unfastened each of the buckets and moved to steady the ladder as Jacob carried them one at a time up the ladder and poured the sloshing sap into the pot.

A newly birthed cloud of steam fogged Jacob's face. "Whew! Looks like sugar harvest this year will be large enough to make plenty of sweets for your fall wedding feast, Polly."

"The way George Schmucker eats, I wouldn't be too sure," laughed John as he tossed some logs on the kettle fire. "Polly'll have to use all of her energy *cooking* after they get married."

"And you won't have enough energy to get back home if you don't stop running your mouth," Polly shot back. "We might just have to leave you out here in the woods to keep the bears company."

"And Ruthie Knepper wouldn't be happy if you got eaten by a bear before next Sunday Meeting," Rebecca added.

John grinned at them. "But she'd sure be smiling if I showed up carrying a bearskin blanket, wouldn't she?"

"Whoa!" Jacob hollered as he backed down the ladder. "I think Ruthie's discovered a better way to keep warm than wrapping up in some smelly old animal hide."

John blushed as red as Jacob's steam-flushed cheeks. Susan nudged Rebecca with her elbow and whispered, "It's sooo *gut* to see John smiling again. Amazing what a *gutes Fräulein* can do."

"Like sunshine after a shower," said Rebecca.

"Enough of that," Daniel barked. But even he couldn't resist a smile. "Syrup's thickened up and ready for the buckets. Fetch the lids."

"Right here, Papa," said Samuel grabbing the wooden tops from the end of the sled.

"*Gut,*" said Daniel. "Children, fill those plates of yours with some fresh snow and get over here."

In an instant the three youngsters scooped a mound of snow onto their saucers and lined up close to their Papa holding them at an arm's length. He went to each in turn and drizzled a generous serving of hot syrup from the ladle onto the cold snow. It cooled immediately into soft candy that they scooped up with their fingers and plopped into their mouths.

By the time Susan got her treat, Cate and Rebecca had already swallowed theirs. Daniel made another round with the same results. "Now, let me fill some buckets before I make any more candy. Polly, John, Jacob – line up for yours next."

"Sounds fair," said Jacob planting himself opposite Cate. Then likewise, Polly and John took their places facing Rebecca and Susan. Only Samuel was left without a partner.

"What about Samuel?" said Rebecca.

"Don't worry about me." Samuel moved to the first bucket filled with syrup and tapped the lid on. "I'll claim this first full bucket instead and share it with Sarah. We'll reheat it at the cabin and make our own sugar candy together after supper."

The cottontail of winter scampered into spring like a jackrabbit running from a hungry fox. Longer days and shorter nights dried the snow-soaked soil enough for turning. Sweet potato plants sprouted in windowsills all across the county. Red potatoes and peas could be planted in four-square gardens later that week on March 17th – St. Gertrude's Day – and the first sowing of wheat and flax was foremost in the minds of local farmers as they greased their wooden or iron plow heads and inspected leather harnesses for tears or signs of weakness. Sleepy winter muscles were itching to be flexed. Cold weather logging, ice harvesting, and making maple syrup, soap and candles all required powerful effort, but nothing like the strength needed to meet the overwhelming demands of planting and harvest.

Sarah sat back on her heels, dropped the hand spade beside her and rested her dirt-caked hands on the swollen belly under her garden apron. She looked across the scatter of dark-brown clods and newly-sprouted weeds framed by the fresh-hewn boards of the four-square garden that Samuel had completed along with their cabin just eight months earlier.

Ten yards away, her sister-in-law Susan was making her second pass at the rows of clumped soil she had dug designated for onion sets, one of the first plantings for the season. She flipped the trowel over in her hand and was pounding at the clods to reduce them to a fine enough texture to ensure a good crop.

"Thank Goodness your mama could spare you to help," said Sarah. "It would take me a week to accomplish what we've done together today." To her left were three long rows of buried peas and a dozen cucumber mounds. After the onions were set, they would spend the rest of the day preparing still more ground for later plantings.

"Especially with a new garden," said Susan wiping her brow with the back of her hand leaving a streak of brown across her forehead shaded from the sun by the bonnet she wore over her cap. "It'll take a few years to have this soil as friendly as what's in our four-square garden at home."

"But Sarah's garden fence is a sight to see," added Rebecca as she dipped the rough straw brush into the pail of whitewash to touch up the last of the spots worn bare by the winter.

"Polly would have come, too, but Mama said for her to stay home to work up a new plot nearer the creek for the extra wedding celery." Susan resumed her task. "If this summer's rain is as sparse as last year's, she won't have as far to tote water. Celery won't last a dry spell."

"And I remember from my own wedding that she needs to get it in the ground as soon as the threat of frost is gone if it's to be ready to harvest by November. It grows as slow as a slug crawls," Sarah said. She stood up awkwardly grabbing her back and pausing to gain her balance. "I'm beginning to feel a little like a slug myself," she groaned. "And the joy in setting our first garden is less knowing that we won't be here for the harvest. I hope whoever leases the ground next month takes proper care of it."

Susan had been thinking the same sad thought most of the day, but had kept silent. *Misery loves company,* she mused, *but I'd rather make Sarah happy than have all of us moping.* "Maybe the soil will be finer in your Cove Forge garden. You'll be able to serve us quite a feast from that harvest when we come to visit."

"Mama will want to come as often as she can manage to see *ihr erstes Enkelkind* and she'll need company for the trip – that would be *Tante* Susan and me," Rebecca declared joining in the effort to cheer Sarah.

"Oh, I hope so," Sarah stammered her eyes glistening. "I pray so every day."

Sensing Sarah's distress, Susan went to the bucket full of spring water hanging on the gate and used the tin cup floating on top to offer her sister-in-law a cool drink. "I know that your mama will be pleased to have you with her those last few months – for the baby and all." She handed Sarah the cup. "Here, taste this. The sun's getting hotter every minute."

Sarah took the cup with both hands and sipped slowly. She couldn't say *danke* without crying – and she knew that Susan understood. Susan also knew that a sisterly hug would only squeeze the tears to the surface, so she just waited.

Finally, Sarah drew in a deep breath and squared her shoulders. "I honestly think it's *amazing* how farm wives can endure such work day after day – season after season. But I will try to be just as *amazing* as the wife of a fine ironmaster and to manage a worthy household of my own – one that *always* has room for guests."

-12-

Signing Day

"Your signature here," said Daniel Royer pointing to the line at the bottom of the legal document before pushing it across the table.

Jonathan Ripple, 23 years old and newly married, stared at the agreement as the quill pen quivered in his hand. *Sweet Jesus,* he thought. *It's all we've got in this world. What if the crop fails? What if a drought comes? What if . . .?"* He sensed Elijah Moore's impatience as he sat beside him waiting to complete the contract on his land. Elijah had already signed and had planting to do back home.

Daniel drummed his calloused fingers and looked outside the open door of his office at the long line of men anxiously waiting their turn. Every April 1st Daniel was bound to his chair as county tax collector administering the official documentation of land leases and renewals in the area. With the recent influx of refugees from the

British threat to the south, business was booming. *Mein Gott,* he fretted silently as the young Ripple continued to ponder. *Make your mark, man. None of us are getting any younger here.* "It's a fine 30 acres and sturdy cabin," he urged. Still the youth hesitated. Daniel leaned toward him. "You can renew the lease or not next April. It's binding for just one year."

Finally, Jonathan steadied his hand long enough to scratch his name and date on the paper. Daniel retrieved it quickly, added his signature on a second line and sprinkled some talc on the document to set the ink. As he blew the excess powder onto the floor and folded the parchment to add to his file he said, "You'll not be sorry. Work hard and the land will serve you well." Then he turned to the door. "Next."

He passed the documents back to David for filing and recording. It would be a long day.

As business continued at the house, a small group of wagons congregated near the barn. Men were delivering the benches and Long Table altar for the Sunday Meeting that the Royers were to host two days later.

John met Edward Lehman as he backed his family's team of horses toward the large double doors. Edward pulled the reins and tied them to the wooden brake arm before stepping over the back of the wagon bench into the bed. John moved behind the wagon and they both grabbed either end of the first of more than a dozen benches. With a shared nod, they lifted it.

"I guess you've already had your share of heaving furniture this week," said John." They moved in tandem lugging their burden toward the doorway. "Is your family all set for the move to Carlisle come Monday?"

"There's not enough room for a flea to sneeze on the wagons," Edward said. "Anything more will have to wait for our first return visit to Waynesburg."

"I know *Susan* will miss seeing you," John said.

They put down the first bench and headed back for the second. Edward hesitated considering his response. "I'll miss Susan, too, but only as I would a sweet younger sister. I hope she's not taken our friendship as something more, though I fear she may have. I hadn't considered *any* girl as more than a friend until . . ."

"Until the snitzen party?" John smiled completing Edward's awkward omission.

"Well . . . ," Edward turned to hide the flush he felt come over his face.

"Don't the Newcomers have family near Carlisle? Some pretty, red-headed cousin, as I recall?" John teased.

Edward surrendered to John's friendly inquisition and raised his eyebrows with a sly grin. "Just a stone's throw away from my Oma's farm – less than two miles." They took hold of the next bench. "Not much farther than the Kneppers' place is from here."

Thinking of Ruthie, John also instantly blushed at Edward's suggestion.

Jacob moved Elsie to a nearby stall to consolidate the livestock's living arrangements and clear an area for the Sunday Meeting. He had caught most of the young men's conversation. "Hey, Edward. It sounds like your new home is located real conveniently for *planting*," he quipped. "Just might yield you quite a pretty *harvest,* huh?"

John kicked some loose straw from the barn floor at his younger brother as he came to Edward's defense. "Well, Jacob, we all know that *you* wouldn't mind having part of our *local crop* for yourself."

Jacob tipped his head as they all three chuckled.

"What's so funny?" asked Samuel arriving from the other end of the barn. "You're all smilin' like raccoons in a henhouse."

"Actually," John answered for all of them. "You could say we're all 'on the prowl.' Right?" He looked to the others who shrugged their shoulders and nodded.

Samuel looked confused, but was too excited about his own news to ask for any more explanation. "I just signed the lease agreement for the cabin and land. It's even more than we dared to hope for. Have you seen Sarah? I can't wait to tell her."

"I think she's with Polly and Susan down by the stream checking on the celery patch for the wedding," said Jacob.

Samuel started to leave, but stopped when he noticed Edward. "Oh, Edward. Your papa's just as pleased as me at what *your* farm brought. Went to a family named Reighart – got at least six children as I counted. Plenty of hands to work the land. We're all sorry to see you go, but this settlement will give your family a good start on their new venture."

"We'll surely miss everyone," Edward shared. "But since Opa Lehman's passing, the dairy farm up north's become too much for Oma and Uncle Aaron. Papa worried mightily about what to do, but the Redcoats' blockade of Baltimore harbor tipped the scales to Carlisle. Said he'd rather deliver milk to Philadelphia in peace than battle the British at Baltimore. Said, 'turning the other cheek is tough enough. Better to move out of the line of fire, if you can.'"

The strained quiet after his remark puzzled Edward who was unaware of John's burning conflict with the issue of the war. Acutely conscious of the tension in the air, John pushed past Samuel and out the door without a word. Jacob turned to Edward. "John's spirit does battle every day with the Redcoats and it's all he can do to keep his body from following. He and Papa have had words about it more than once."

"I didn't realize," Edward apologized.

"Not many outside of our family do," Jacob explained. "We hoped he was beginning to find some peace, but yesterday a teamster brought news from Baltimore of the terrible suffering the

148

British have caused. Papa has banned all talk and news of the war from the house, but the air's full of it."

"Well, the air I feel today is full of *good* tidings and I mean to share them with Sarah," Samuel declared. "I'll be back to help you as soon as I do."

"She's gonna catch cold," Susan warned. "Just look at her lower lip shaking. The water's too cold for wading, even if the sun's warmer than usual."

"Don't worry so much. *Sei nicht so ein Pessimist*," Polly crowed from her perch barefooted and ankle-deep in the early spring rush of the creek. She was linked hand in hand to two-year-old Nan who was balancing on a flat rock in the creek bed that allowed barely an inch of the stream to splash across her wiggling toes." Polly leaned over to her little sister. "Are you cold? Do you want to get out?"

"N-n-n-no," Nan stuttered. Her big, brown eyes begged. "I w-w-wanna th-th-thtay here. P-p-p--pleath, P-p-p-Polly."

Polly looked triumphantly at Susan. "No, p-p-p-problem, Nan. You're a hardy girl like me. A little chill will never ruin our fun."

Susan shook her head and moved up the soggy bank to Sarah who was watching from the edge of Polly's garden where the celery was just pushing up through the ground. "I think Polly takes too many chances," Susan said, "but she's right about having fun. She has always been *sehr gut* at that."

"I'm more like you, Susan," said Sarah, "but Samuel has Polly's bold streak. He's so excited about starting work on Monday at that new iron forge – about learning all he can to become an ironmaster. He says 'the local Scotch-Irish and Welsh are making the northern iron furnaces as grand as the southern cotton plantations.'

"He's starting as a collier, making charcoal from timber. Nearly 1,000 cords of wood cut last winter are waiting when he gets to the job. Gabriel Calimer will be working with him to stand the heavy, four-foot logs on end in a big circle, three tiers high with a six-foot wide hole in the middle – like a cone around a chimney. Samuel told me they'll have to cover the stacking with dirt and debris. Then they lay a thick, notched log from the base of the heap to the edge of the hole so they can climb to the top and drop in some kindling to start the smoldering.

"Samuel and Gabriel will have to watch it day and night for five days so it doesn't catch flame and ruin the charcoal transformation. They'll stay in an old cabin with the open door facing the smoke the whole time. After that, it takes ten days to cool, harvest and load the charcoal – and then they start all over again.

Susan sighed. "Good thing you've moved to town with your family. You'd be so lonely by yourself on those days that he's gone all night long."

I'll still miss him," Sarah said. "But even more, his job is so dangerous. What if that huge pile collapses or the fire gets out of control? What if he loses his balance walking up the notched log? What if one of those powerful Kentucky mules they use to haul the finished charcoal to the furnace rears up and stomps him? What if . . .?"

Susan hugged Sarah. "'What-if's' are like weeds, Sarah. They're everywhere, especially where you don't want them. The gears at the gristmill, acid at the tannery – remember when Rebecca's dress caught fire at the kiln last year? We just have to hold on to wisdom and faith in God. Samuel and Polly have both wisdom and faith and they're a bit braver than you and me."

Polly tramped up the slope with Nan propped on her hip. They plopped down together on a grassy spot and pulled on their socks and shoes. Sarah lowered herself slowly beside Nan, picked up one of her tiny, chilled feet and nestled it gently into her small sock. *It won't be long until my little one is as big as she is,* she thought feeling a strong kick from beneath her ribs. She shimmied a little soft leather shoe over the sock. "Does that feel better?"

"Yeth," lisped Nan flinging her arms around Sarah's neck almost knocking her backward.

Sarah soaked in the feel of the child's arms hugging her. *Lord, help me to be a good mother.*

Polly watched the two giggling together on the grass. *Lord, help me to be a good wife.*

Susan took in the whole scene washed in spring sunshine and love. *Lord, help me to trust that life is changing as it should, even if it scares me sometimes.*

"Sarah!" Samuel called from the top of the field. She stood and turned to watch him running toward her. Nan toddled off in his direction with her arms in the air. He whisked her up and planted her on his shoulders. "Hang on!" he said galloping to a stop beside his wife. "Good news! We got more than we ever expected for the farm lease. All the papers are signed and sealed."

"*Wundervoll,*" she cheered. She wrapped her arm around his waist and walked him toward the freshly cultivated plot nearby. "Just look at Polly's wedding celery."

Feathery yellow-green shoots peeked like eyelashes at them through the soil. "Looks like the crop has a healthy start – just like us," said Samuel kissing her cheek. Polly and Susan strolled over to meet them.

By noon, the line waiting outside Daniel's office was no shorter. Work continued in the summer kitchen, as well, with preparations for the noon meal.

Cate zipped around the corner of the door. "Look, Mama. Ten eggs today! The hens are really getting into spring laying." She relished her newest solo responsibility of checking the nesting boxes every day. Susan and Rebecca had completed her training during the slower laying phase of the winter months.

Catherine admired the brown ovals nestled carefully in the gathering basket that Cate had put on the work table littered with purple turnip tops and curled apple peels, smeared utensils and dripping bowls. "Can't happen too soon for the hungry mouths around here," Catherine said. She peered out the open window at the bustle of activity on the farm framed by blue skies and clouds of wispy mare's tails. The brass weathervane at the peak of the barn danced in the westerly breeze as if celebrating the glorious day.

Elizabeth sat at the far end of the longer table in the summer kitchen arranging two slices of apple pie atop two covered bowls of cooked turnips and salt pork in a sizeable oak basket lined with a linen towel. She wedged two tankards along the sides to secure the contents and folded the cloth across the top.

"Is it ready?" asked Rebecca standing behind her.

"*Ja*," said Elizabeth turning around on the bench and resting the substantial packed meal on her lap. "Papa and David will be eating with one hand and writing with the other today. I'm sure that the corn mush and molasses they ate before sunup is a distant memory by now."

Rebecca grasped the thick handle with both hands. "It's heavy," she said as she lifted it toward her. "I'll have to deliver this first and make a second trip with the cider pitcher."

"Go through the house instead of the back yard," Elizabeth directed. "Too many folks to weave through waiting at the back door to do business."

"It'll be a late supper tonight by the look of it. We may have to light the candles at the table when we finally sit down together in the dining room," said Catherine.

Rebecca took her first steps, carefully balancing her payload.

Catherine watched her leave. "Now that those two men are on their way to being fed, we'd best clear the big table for the crowd that's helping in the barn. It'll be good to visit for a time with Samuel and Sarah." Catherine wiped her hands on her apron as Cate shuffled dirty dishes and pans to the washbasin. Elizabeth stacked clean plates, spoons and mugs from the shelf onto the table where there was space.

Content that the simmering pots on the stove and the platters of bread and sweets were sufficient for the impending noon meal, Catherine retrieved a large kettle from the hook on the rafter above the stove. "Now for the soup." She suspended the pot from the wrought-iron swing arm of the large hearth and poured in three two-gallon crocks of dried beans and pitcher after pitcher of spring water from the kitchen pump. "*Ist gut* the host family provides only the soup for Sunday Meeting meal. These beans should be soaked and softened enough to add the ham hocks and hang over the fire after we've finished eating."

As the third full pitcher of cider took the last available opening on the board, Polly stepped outside and rang the large brass bell hanging from the eave. Jacob, John and Edward arrived while the bell was still vibrating – the rest weren't far behind.

As the quarter moon rose among the twinkling stars that night, a sense of reverence settled over the quiet barn anticipating the transformation to come. Sunday morning, a hundred or more Brethren would enter to begin their Sabbath with three to four hours of communal worship. The benches were lined up on either side of the central aisle that led to the highly polished Long Table where the deacons would deliver their messages.

The ink had dried and wax had cooled with the imprints of legal stamps on documents that could transform lives. For Daniel and David Royer, one of the year's longest days was ending.

Alles war in Ordnung in preparation for a Sunday devoted more to prayer than to work. Many of the daily household chores would be completed in advance of the Sabbath – wood stacked –

foods prepared and stored – and all other tasks put aside to begin anew on Monday.

As Catherine had predicted, candlelight lit the weary faces of her family as they finished the day's final meal. The scrapes and scratches of eating the modest offering echoed in the silence of the dining room. Conversations had wrung out and given way to solitary musings.

Jacob skewered the last bite of sausage and chewed it slowly. Despite his fatigue, he wanted with every ounce of his being to tell them – to tell his family what had been burning in his heart since the day he saw Elizabeth in Papa's sickroom. *But what about John?* He stole a glance at his best friend. They were so unlike each other in appearance and temperament, but for as long as either of them could remember, they had been inseparable. *If I say that I'm ready, that I truly want to be baptized, John's hesitation will look even worse. He's already so upset about the war. I can't do that to him, but now that I know what I feel, the waiting is horrible.*

"Can I be excused?" Jacob asked his father.

"*Ja,*" Daniel replied.

"*Kann ich auch gehen?*" asked John.

Daniel rose from his seat. "You are *all* excused when you are ready. Devotions will be early tonight before we're too tired to

156

give the Lord our full attention. One hour, in the parlor." He raised his eyebrows at Catherine. "Can the necessary chores be done by then?"

"*Ja, mein Mann.*"

"*Gut,*" he pronounced. "*Immer gut, meine Frau.*"

-13-

Harbingers of Harvest

In the day-to-day of living, time crawls, but as season rolls to season, it flies. Daylight no sooner stretches to the fullness of summer, than it begins to shrink as a harbinger of the harvest.

Five months of nature's progress had marched across the Royer farmstead. Bean vines had crept up and over the four-square garden fence while the raised beds overflowed with an ongoing bounty of vegetables and herbs. Spring corn kernels lovingly swaddled in soil had become tassel-topped stalks spiked with full ears spouting strands of silk. Plentiful summer showers had urged the celery crop to a generous proportion for Polly's wedding.

Easter had come and gone. The youngest Royers filled the nests they had fashioned from straw with colorful spring flowers and left them in the garden for the Easter Rabbit on Saturday evening. Sometime that night he had hidden beautiful eggs for the children to find after Sunday worship.

The bustling farmstead was a feast for the senses – the continual grumble of the unceasing gristmill crushing fresh-cut wheat and rye to flour, the slow buzz of once pesky flies grown lethargic with late summer doldrums, the chirp of crickets that accompanied the flash of lightning bugs in the warm night air. Honeycombs in bee trees dripped with sweetness, the icehouse harvest was reduced by half under piles of dampened sawdust and the farmstead was drenched in the intense odors of the stagnant brew of the tannery and privy. Late August was bursting with ripeness.

The curtains of the big, stone house were perpetually drawn against the sun and every meal was shared in the coolness of the summer kitchen. Polly's *kist* brimmed with many of the necessities to adorn the small, shuttered house in town that George had purchased just weeks before. The sharply defined tan lines tattooed on the men's foreheads were revealed when they hung their hats on the pegs at day's end. Nan's more complex sentences had lost their lisp and the seams of Susan's bodice showed more signs of strain every day. Ezra Provines had applied the last coat of black walnut stain to the cradle he crafted for his first grandchild out of oak slabs from his cooperage, and Samuel had labored as collier, quarrier and filler, in turn, learning step-by-step his ironmaster trade in the blasting heat of Mont Alto Furnace.

Twenty Sunday Meetings had passed since the Lehmans departed for Carlisle. Last week's Sunday Meeting was hosted by the Reigharts, who had successfully completed their assimilation into the congregation and adoption of the land they had purchased from the Lehmans five months earlier.

The circuit had come full circle since April. In three days the Royers would again host Sunday Meeting. The event would be a virtual replay of the last as they fulfilled each required item in turn. Only one key difference held a special significance for the Royers this time. The baptism – Jacob's baptism – would take place right after this Sunday's service down by the small wooden bridge built by his Opa Stoner more than 50 years before, the same setting as the baptisms of his two older brothers and sisters.

John and Jacob felt the dual rhythm of their wheat harvest labor as easily as they did their own heartbeats. The swish of the scythe, the loop and latch of the twine around the sheath, the heave and catch to the wagon bed made a symphony of motion. Dusty clouds of chaff hung in the air and acres of golden stubble fell in behind them as one by one they stacked the tall bundles in the wagon.

John hugged the newest swath of wheat together as Jacob wound the twine twice around, secured it and cut it with his work blade. "Hope we can finish this ten acres today," said John picking up the long-handled scythe. We'll be losing harvest time tomorrow to setup for Sunday Meeting."

Jacob surveyed what remained uncut. "We've reaped more than this in less time before."

John made several passes with the razor sharp blade. He paused in anticipation of Jacob's usual help in assembling the cuts, but Jacob hesitated. When John looked back to investigate, Jacob stood with his arms crossed over his chest and stared back at him. "You've said nothing about it, *Bruder*."

John held Jacob's eyes for a split-second. They both understood the meaning behind the accusation before John hung his head.

"Nothing," Jacob repeated. At John's silence, he continued, "I'd rather have you hit me – yell at me. Anything but silence. You're like a stranger instead of a brother."

"Envy stops me, Jacob. I've been praying to get rid of it, but its hook's set deep and I can't shake it." He lowered himself onto the end of the wagon bed beside his younger brother. "I realize you waited months to tell everyone you wanted to be baptized because you saw how I was struggling. I knew you were waiting, but I said nothing because your devotion made me envy you even more."

Jacob sighed. "I didn't want to cause you any more trouble. I didn't want Papa to use *my* request to criticize *your* hesitation."

"I know. I've known all of your reasons all along," John pleaded. "*Du bist der beste Mann* – the best man I know. But what could – can – I do? My doubts keep fighting with my spirit. I want to say what you want to hear, but I don't want to lie."

"Just don't hate me, John. Be my friend. That's more important than our differences."

"I could never hate you."

"Then you don't need to say anything else. *Du bist auch ein guter Mann,* John. I can't imagine the battle you're fighting, but I'll always care about you. Share your troubles with me. Talk about them and we can face them together."

John cradled his head in his hands. Neither brother moved for a time as they absorbed the weight of their conversation. Finally he looked up and the brothers shared a heartfelt embrace. "I'll celebrate your baptism this Sunday with as much true spirit as I can muster," he pledged.

"And I'll celebrate our friendship," said Jacob slapping John on the back. "Now this wheat's still waiting for us. Let's get to it."

Sarah barely managed to sit still on the hard bench during the long hours of the Sunday service. Sweat dripped from many a brow and fans flapped steadily as the stagnant humidity of the day mixed with the body heat of close to 80 Brethren in the confines of the barn. After the final 'Amen,' Samuel came over to Sarah from the men's side of the center aisle knowing she would appreciate a balancing arm to help her look less clumsy when she tried to stand. As she reached to take hold of his arm and pull herself upright, she winced and grabbed her hip pushing the heel of her free hand against the small of her back for support.

"I warned you yesterday that you were overdoing it with all of that packing," Samuel scolded. "Looks like you're paying the price today."

"But I felt fine doing it, Samuel. Soon I won't have as much time for things like that," she objected.

Sarah's mother stood up beside her and tapped Catherine who sat in front of them. "I recall those unusual bursts of energy close to my time, don't you, Catherine?"

"*Ja, genau so.* Very close to my time, all ten times." She smiled at Sarah and Samuel. "You shouldn't be waiting much longer now. Keep a firm hold on Samuel's arm as you make your way down to the stream. It's a little rough going in places."

Susan and Rebecca followed their family down the hill past the Fahnestocks' house and four-square garden toward the half-mile trail that led to the familiar spot by the Antietam Creek where Jacob and the other aspirant, 16-year-old Mary Reighart, waited on the creek bank with the bishop for the rest of the congregation to arrive.

John was just a pace apart from the family – one of them, but a shade distant, a tear in the family fabric that few, if any, noticed other than those who knew his situation.

Despite the significance of the proceedings, Susan couldn't help but notice Mary Reighart's 14-year-old brother Henry with his family walking just a few feet ahead of her. *He's nearly as tall as his father already. And what a long stride to his step – confident, but not proud.*

Rebecca was quick to notice Susan's distraction. She tugged on her sister's sleeve and whispered, "Better to keep your eyes on your own brother instead of Mary's today."

They shared a secret smile as they joined hands and searched ahead for a glimpse of Bishop Martin and the aspirants.

The arched tree limbs crowded with deep green leaves drooped high overhead enveloping the soft burble of the creek and occasional twitter of finches. Crystalline reflections in the water were distorted by the ripple of the current as it swept along under the stone buttresses of the small wooden bridge.

The Royer and Reighart families moved forward through the wide semi-circle of solemn spectators to the space reserved for them nearest the creek bank.

Bishop Martin stood tall in his high-collared white shirt and simple black vest beside the two aspirants robed in white with their heads slightly bowed. All three were barefoot in preparation for the sacrament to come. The bishop stretched his neck to survey the crowd and confirm that the necessary parties had arrived.

Content that all were present, he waded ankle-deep into the creek and nodded at Mary and Jacob inviting them to come and stand on either side of him. "Beloved Brethren," he began lifting his arms toward the sky. "Our Lord has provided this serene sanctuary of nature on this glorious day to welcome these two blessed children into our fellowship of believers. It is with joy and reverence that. . ."

Mary, being a year older than Jacob, was the first to wade further out and join the bishop in the deeper water rising well above their knees. She knelt beside him facing upstream, folded her hands over her heart, closed her eyes and bowed her head.

"Dear Lord," the bishop prayed fervently. "Your daughter Mary comes to you willingly today to commit her soul to You and her devotion to our faith community. As the blood of our Savior cleansed us of our sins, as the prophet John baptized our Savior with water, so today . . . Amen."

The bishop placed his hand on Mary's head and dipped her face forward under the flowing water three times announcing in turn, "I baptize you in the name of the Father . . . the Son . . . and the Holy Spirit."

"Amen," the company of believers intoned in unison.

The bishop helped Mary to her feet and she exchanged places with Jacob. She waited, her wet robes plastered to her and water dripping from her tightly bound bun and long eyelashes, as Jacob knelt beside the bishop.

"Dear Lord," Bishop Martin repeated, "your son Jacob comes to you willingly today . . . Amen."

The bishop immersed Jacob as he had Mary only moments before. A warm peace arose in Catherine, a glow that filled her head behind her closed eyes and wrapped around her heart. Though this was her fifth child to be baptized, the memory of such joy never equaled the intensity of experiencing it anew.

"Amen," the witnesses responded once again.

The final prayers were said as the drenched aspirants received their blessing. The bishop excused them to hurry to the Fahnestocks' nearby farmhouse where their dry change of clothes waited.

"Now back to the house and the feast," Catherine announced awash in the moment. The crowd afforded the Royers and the Reigharts the lead position on the path for the return trip.

Cate scampered up behind her mother and grabbed her hand. "Mama, I can't find Samuel and Sarah."

Catherine's pulse began to race as she glanced at the company behind her, but she could see little. "Polly," she called.

Impatient with no immediate response, she called again louder, "Polly!"

Daniel turned around, "What's wrong, Catherine? Why the shouting?"

"Where are Samuel and Sarah? They would never miss Jacob's baptism, not unless . . ."

Before Daniel could react, Polly came running up to them. "Oh, Mama – Papa. Frau Knepper just told me. Halfway down the path coming to the baptism, Sarah asked Samuel to fetch her mother and said that they had best get to town quickly. Oh, Mama, do you think . . .?"

She hugged Polly. "Yes, I surely do!" She turned to Daniel. "*Mein Mann*, it appears that the Lord would have us celebrate two births today. Jacob's been born into the fellowship, but *unser erstes Enkelkind*, our first grandchild, will soon be born to the world."

"*Gott zu loben.* Praise God," said Daniel obviously pleased but tempering his reaction to maintain his staunch masculinity.

Elizabeth rushed over. "Mama, I just heard. You and Papa go ahead into town as soon as we get home. I'll stay back with the girls. We can handle the meal."

Before Catherine could respond, *Frau* Reighart was beside them. The news had flown through the crowd. "*Frau und Herr* Royer, your children will have plenty of hands to help with the noon meal and the farm. Godspeed you to town. *Alles ist hier gut.*"

"Vielen Dank," said Catherine as Daniel added a somber appreciative nod.

John called out as he sped past his father, "I'll saddle Elsie for you, Papa. And hitch a team to the wagon for Mama and me. Meet you at the barn."

-14-

Trouble in Town

"Slow down girl, don't drink so fast," said John as he patted the shiny wet coat of Maggie, the older of the two horses who had pulled the wagon from the Royer farmstead to Waynesburg at a pace the old horses hadn't run in years. He could feel the rhythm of the mare's heart and the steam rising from her damp hide. "You never want to get in the way of an Oma-to-be who's determined to get there afore her grandbaby's born, now do ya' girl?"

John kept an eye on the amount of water the horses slurped from the trough at the pump near the Provines' barn. From the instant his mother learned of Samuel and Sarah's hurried departure from the baptism, Catherine had moved with the haste of an agile young woman. She had practically jumped from the wagon and was through the Provines' front door before he'd even had a chance to halt the horses. He was surprised his mother with strands of silver edging her bonnet could move that quickly, especially in her long skirt. He heard no high-pitched cries from the house and he could tell from Samuel and Daniel's pacing outside that the baby had not yet arrived.

Catherine said nary a word, but squeezed the expectant father's elbow reassuringly and kissed her husband's cheek as she breezed into the house.

"You might as well go tend the horses, John," said Samuel looking as helpless as John had ever seen him. "They tell me it'll be awhile. Even so, I'd best stay here."

"I'm pretty sure nothing could drag any of you away. Tell Mama I'll be back in a few hours to check. I'll be keeping all of you in my prayers."

"Thank you, brother – or should I say 'uncle.'" They both smiled as John urged the horses to the Provines' nearby carriage shed and Samuel resumed his vigil.

John was relieved to have a mission and more than happy to turn his attention to creatures he understood. Horses, cows, goats and kittens were one thing – the newest little Royer was quite another. Farm animals gave birth easily in time with the seasons, but when he asked his mother how long they'd be in town for this birth, all she'd said was 'Babies come when they are good 'n ready and not a moment before.'

Once the horses' breathing slowed, John tied the reins to the hitching post beside Elsie, still lathered from Daniel's trip, and gave all of them a handful of grain as a reward. Their rough tongues tickled the hollow of his palm sending a tingle up his spine. "It's been quite a day for the Royers," he told Maggie as she nosed his hand hoping for more food. "First Jacob's baptism and now Samuel and Sarah's new baby."

John dipped into the feed bin after more grain for the horses. As they lapped it up and crushed it with their teeth like the loud grinding stones of the gristmill, he sensed a commotion on the other side of 'the Diamond' some distance down the main street of town. In the sticky humidity his ears caught wind of a disturbance. Men were shouting and, as he walked closer, he saw women clustered in the dusty street behind them. Everyone was talking at once. *It might be powerful hot,* thought John as he stepped up his pace, *but I'll wager this uproar has nothing to do with the weather and everything to do with the Redcoats.*

As he came within earshot, he heard a crimson-faced Silas McBride shouting, "I tell you they'll be headin' our way next. First the Bloody Brits burn The President's House and now they've attacked Fort McHenry. Those Lobsterbacks will come marchin' up the Baltimore Turnpike right through Waynesburg before you know it, and then we'll all be runnin' for our lives!"

"Now, Silas," said Patrick Mooney in a calm, but firm voice. "The militias are holding off the Redcoats and America will prevail. The British are no match for us on our home ground. Didn't we prove that last time fellas?" he said scanning the restless crowd. Many waved broadsheets that had just arrived by post rider bearing the latest accounts of the British Army's fiery rampage through Washington and news of the relentless naval assault on Baltimore. He gave John a nod of recognition as the young man joined the ranks of those congregating outside the White Swan Tavern.

As the rumbling of the crowd grew, John felt his face flush. *Vater won't even talk about the war. All he does, even with these latest threats, is bark out orders to step up production of all the grain, hides, butter and crops we can manage. He shouts 'Wer rastet, der rostet,' over and over. Every time he preaches 'he who rests, rusts,' it turns my stomach.*

John's jaw clenched as he recalled the gleam in his father's eyes at the mention of the high price their goods were fetching. *He cares more about profits than stopping the British rats*, he thought.

Days earlier, when word came that British troops had entered Washington and torched many of the federal government's buildings, including the big white house President Madison and his wife had just moved into, John felt a rage he had never known. His first impulse was to take down the Pennsylvania rifle from over the fireplace mantle in his father's back office and enlist in a militia that was being organized in Mercersburg. The accounts of Dolley Madison and her slaves loading up wagons with the house's treasures and abandoning the newly-completed president's mansion to the will of the British troops staggered him.

Thankfully, Mrs. Madison had the presence of mind to take the full-length portrait of George Washington with her, saving it from the flames that soon engulfed the house, the Congressional building and nearly every public structure in Washington City. John imagined the panic and horror that would ensue if the British were to come to their Franklin County farmstead and burn *their* new home. He wondered if anyone would think to take *their* painting of George Washington from over the kitchen hearth if they had to flee for their lives.

If they can burn Washington, what can't they do? John fumed silently as he walked the perimeter of the angry circle. He heard excited threats against the British soldiers and boasts of patriots unafraid of British bayonets. But he also heard Michael Corkery, the most successful businessman in town, talking quietly about what might happen if the Redcoats won. "England's war with Napoleon is over now," he said to the men beside him. "That'll just give the Crown more ships and men to throw against us. We have no other course, to be sure," he said, "but the British lion could certainly give its young cub a drubbing. Our fighting spirit is one thing, but the might of the Royal Navy is quite another."

The townsfolk's openness as they discussed the war with Britain struck John. It was not so at the Royers. A fierce glare from his father, a sharp look and raised eyebrow from his mother and the hush of everyone within earshot accompanied any mention of the conflict. The subject of this latest war with England was clearly *verboten* at home.

The only time he could recall his father addressing the issue was the day *Herr* Fahnestock had come to pay his taxes in the back room of the house. 'I wonder when this war will end?' their tenant miller had asked in passing,

With scarcely a pause in his counting, Daniel had snapped. *'Alles hat ein Ende, nur die Wurst hat zwei.'*

'Ach, Herr Royer, that's a good one,' *Herr* Fahnestock had laughed. 'You are so right. Everything does have an end. Only the sausage has two.'

As John eased past Mr. Corkery, brushing up against the large stones of the tavern's wall, he noticed a group of young men gathered across the dirt street listening to an elderly man in an old-fashioned tricorn hat. John recognized him immediately. *He's one of the ''76 men' – he fought with John Wallace and "Mad" Anthony Wayne in the Revolution,* John remembered.

"We walloped the British in '76. Now it's up to you young'uns to carry on the fight," the man said. "Cap'n John Flanagan from Mercersburg is raisin' a company and you fellas should sign up. Our country could use a good strappin' lad like you," the whiskered gentlemen said, pointing to Isaac Hughes. "Chambersburg men are already up in New York fightin' along the Canadian border. They had to go up there 'cause we can't count on the New Englanders to do their part. Them cod fishers didn't support this war from the beginnin', so it's up to us Pennsylvanians to defend our country. Now with the attack on Washington, Flanagan's gonna lead them Mercersburg boys over South Mountain and show those Brits in Bal'imer how we frontier men fight!"

Before John could slip away, the old man caught his eye and called out to him, "How 'bout you, son? Bet you're a good shot."

"Oh, he's a good shot all right. That John Royer can take a rabbit at 100 yards in heavy fog," said Isaac before John could protest. "But he's not allowed, him bein' a Dunker'n all. Them 'black hats' ain't allowed to fight. His daddy'd probably be right ready to pay the four dollars the law says they'd owe the militia to 'low John here to stay home and work."

John's face reddened under the brim of his hat as everyone turned to look. *Get away from me. I feel bad enough already, Isaac,* John pleaded silently.

But Isaac continued his assault. "You don't fight, do ya, Johnny boy?" he taunted. John squinted his loathing at Isaac before turning to escape the muffled ridicule of the others.

The only relief John felt that day came later when Samuel shared the news of the healthy arrival of his son.

In the quiet of his room that night, despite the family's happiness over Jacob's baptism and jubilation surrounding the safe birth of the Royers' first grandchild, John closed his eyes tight and covered his ears to shut out the memory of Isaac's stinging words. In a fitful sleep he replayed the scene of Jacob's baptism and awoke to find tears of both joy and despair on his cheeks.

Two weeks later Catherine announced her intention to spend the afternoon with Sarah and her new grandchild, a tiny pink squiggle, also named Daniel. John volunteered to take her to town, anything to remove himself from proximity to his father.

While the womenfolk visited at the Provines', he walked down Main Street toward the general store. Several men were gathered on the porch around Francis McKeon, the reed-thin schoolmaster who supplemented his meager teaching salary using his calligraphy and artistic skills to create *Taufscheine* and

Frakturen – the colorfully decorated marriage, birth and baptismal certificates that his German neighbors prized so highly.

John listened with the others as the schoolteacher read aloud portions of a poem printed in a recently delivered broadsheet. A Marylander named Francis Scott Key from Frederick had written the lines about the bombardment of Fort McHenry he had witnessed in the Battle of Baltimore. The verse had spread like a fierce wind throughout the country. America's terrible suffering in that fierce confrontation became very clear in the teacher's measured cadence:

> *Oh, say can you see by the dawn's early light*
> *What so proudly we hailed at the twilight's last gleaming?*
> *Whose broad stripes and bright stars through the perilous fight,*
> *O'er the ramparts we watched were so gallantly streaming?*
> *And the rocket's red glare, the bombs bursting in air,*
> *Gave proof through the night that our flag was still there.*
> *Oh, say does that star-spangled banner yet wave*
> *O'er the land of the free and the home of the brave?*

When the reading ended everyone was silent, lost in their private thoughts. John stood in the back of the store thinking, *I can't believe that Papa ignores how important it is to fight the British. He's just using our faith as an excuse to keep me from enlisting.* John turned away from the others, ashamed of his inability to take up the cause they supported. *Papa's such a hypocrite! He was a ranger himself in the Revolution and brags about how he and Opa Royer helped General Washington at Valley Forge, but he won't let me serve now.*

John had turned this over and over in his mind while working the fields. He wrestled daily with what the church elders taught and his family believed – that war was wrong and the Brethren way was one of peace. His mind was filled with questions. The Old Testament lessons were full of armies smiting other armies. Didn't the biblical David, a farm boy not much different than himself, bring Goliath to his knees? How was defending the country any different now? The deacons had reminded the congregants time and time again that the way of God is not the way of man and that their own bitter experience with princes in Europe long ago had taught them to stay away from temporal affairs. Still, John struggled.

As the words of Key's moving poem ran though his head, John became acutely conscious of the weight of his black hat, a clear confirmation of his Brethren heritage. Much of the doctrine rang true for him, but this call to avoid such an enemy rankled. He clenched his fists as he thought with contempt.

As he felt the sweat raised by the afternoon sun trickle down the back of his neck, he recalled his promise to be at the Provines' after the noon meal to take his mother home. He made his way in that direction just as he heard Catherine calling from the wooden sidewalk in front of the dry goods store only a few blocks from where she had been cuddling her new grandson.

"John," she announced as they caught sight of each other. "I didn't expect to have to go all over town to find you. We need to get home now."

"Sorry, Mama," he said as he stepped up onto the planks beside her. "I got caught up in the ruckus about how we beat the Brits at Baltimore." Her slight frown at the highly charged topic prompted him to add quickly, "Schoolmaster McKeon received a new broadsheet and he read a wonderful poem by a man named Key from Frederick who was inspired at the battle. Everyone who . . ."

"Well, I prefer to be *inspired* by my beautiful new grandson," said Catherine cutting him off mid-sentence.

"He's a charmer, I agree," said John picturing the wriggling baby he had seen earlier. He thought to himself, *Why in heaven's name did Samuel and Sarah name their innocent son after someone as cold and hateful as Papa?*

"You can wait here, Mama. I'll get the wagon and we can get going."

-15-

Polly's Wedding

George Schmucker ran his hand across the smooth cool plaster wall that framed one of the two double-hung front windows of the modest weatherboard and brick home that would soon be his and Polly's. *Two days – just two days*, he thought. George had used all of his carpentry skills and brothers' help to make the dwelling special. His sister had sewn the homespun curtains that he pushed aside to take in the view of the narrow lane that bordered their small front yard just a block from Main Street. The tall oak shading the front porch was tinged a deep, October red.

He crossed the room and crouched by the large stone hearth – the heart of the house – and made some minor adjustments in the stack of split logs and kindling awaiting its first lighting. "That's better," he said.

The slat-backed oak rocker from his uncle's wood shop sat near the fireplace inviting him to sit and ponder. He rocked slowly, trying to grasp the reality of it all. "I can't remember when I didn't love her." He drew the prized handkerchief from his pocket and ran his fingers over her embroidery – the 'PR' and heart on one corner and the 'GS' on the other – recalling the day she had given it to him secretly behind the Fahnestocks' barn. *Nearly three years ago. The setting sun that day set her red hair – and my heart – on fire.*

Moving to the cherry mantle he had lovingly carved, polished and placed over the hearth, he draped the delicate swatch of linen in the center and smoothed it straight. "I swore to myself that I would carry this until we were married. It'll look perfect right here . . . in two days." He folded the handkerchief and tucked it back in his pocket. *In just two days' time, she'll be my wife.* He smiled.

A knock at the door jarred him to the present. "Come in," he called as he made his way to welcome his visitor.

Jacob stuck his head in the door. "Greetings, *Bruder*. John and I have a delivery for you." He turned his back to the open door and bent down. "Ready, John? Heave." Jacob stood slowly with his hands hooked under the bottom edge of Polly's *kist* – the one that she had been filling with household goods since childhood – and

181

started shuffling backwards into the room under its weight. John followed supporting his end a shade higher given his six-inch height advantage.

"Where do you want this, George?" asked John.

"*Hier ist gut.*" He pointed at the wall just inside the door. "I'm sure Polly knows exactly where she wants it, but I don't. I'll move it to suit her later."

The brothers lowered the chest in place and stood up turning their heads to get a sweeping view of the room. "*Gute Arbeit.* You've done a fine job here, George," said John.

"*Danke,*" said George. "My new family's been a great help."

Jacob shook his head in agreement with John as he assessed the detailing on the mantle. "No wonder Polly's been smiling so much lately."

"And we thought she was thinking about the wedding night," John laughed slapping George on the back.

"Well, maybe that, too," Jacob added as George blushed. "Mama sent us on some last minute errands for the wedding and Polly insisted that we bring this along."

"And when Polly insists, it's best just to do as she says," John said. "Though I'm sure you already know that, right George?"

George smiled. "I certainly admire her spirit."

"We've got plenty of wedding 'spirit' flying around at home. It's got everybody jumping," said Jacob.

"Have you got time for a mug of cider?" George offered.

"*Nein, danke.* If we aren't back home before supper, Mama will have our hides," said John.

"If Polly doesn't get to us first," Jacob added grasping George's shoulder. "George, we've felt like you're our brother for a long time. It'll be our honor to make it official on Thursday."

"Amen," said John.

"And my honor, too," said George.

Polly's wedding day dawned crisp and bright. The Royer farmstead was a beehive of activity preparing to host nearly 200 people at the marriage of Daniel Royer's second daughter – the first of his six girls to wed.

Polly and Elizabeth stood facing each other in their bedroom as Elizabeth, with tears creeping down her cheeks, inspected the ties of Polly's sparkling white bridal cape. "Stop blubbering," scolded Polly. "I'm only moving to town, not . . . ." Her voice cracked and her eyes began to pool as well.

Elizabeth was barely two years older than Polly. Neither girl could recall life without the other. Sandwiched between two sets of brothers, the exceptional bond between the girls was inevitable. They had grown up always together, but had developed personalities and attitudes that were worlds apart. Rather than divide them, not unlike polar ends of magnets, their starkly opposite natures forged an enduring bond.

Catherine caught a glimpse of her two oldest daughters as she swept by their bedroom door on her quest to retrieve some fresh lavender from a vase in the front bedroom to add to Polly's bridal bouquet. She paused, unseen, and thought, *What a special pair. So different, but always so close.*

Polly – practical Polly with her red curly hair and strong frame – faced the realities of life head-on. She was quick to speak her mind and act on her impulses. The limitations of her gender and belief often grated on her, but she emerged from her early self-conflict strong in her resolve and firmly grounded in her world. No one, not even George, understood her as well as Elizabeth.

Elizabeth – ethereal Elizabeth with her straight chestnut brown hair and lanky figure – embraced the spiritual realm. She was a quiet and reflective observer of life and servant of God, but as strong in this resolve as Polly was in hers. She put her questions to God and found peace and purpose in this connection. Only Polly could connect with the Elizabeth solely of *this* world – devoid of her spiritual veil.

They would miss each other.

An autumn breeze swept an eddy of dry leaves across the stone path as Susan made her way from the summer kitchen to the milk house to fetch yet another square of butter for her mother. Despite the monumental planning and early preparations, the day's tasks would pause only for the three-hour ceremony. Rebecca flew past Susan with yet another offering for the sweets table that was already bowing from the weight of the platters.

As Susan reached for the iron ring on the heavy wooden milk house door, she paused to study the web of barbed branches heavy with rust-red berries clinging to the stone wall. *Bittersweet*, she thought. She snapped off a small cluster of the berries and laid them in her palm. "Just like today – bittersweet," she said.

She pulled one of the berries away from the bunch and pictured Samuel and Sarah's tightly packed wagon set to depart for Cove Forge the next day – the tiny bubbles at the corner of infant Daniel's rosebud mouth. "One gone," she said. Then she detached another berry recalling Polly's new home in town. "Two gone." She considered pulling loose yet a third but paused. "John – poor John. He suffers so here." She let all of the pieces sift between her fingers to the ground. "It feels like our family's dissolving."

Then she shook her head to adjust her thinking. "But today is only 'sweet.' Sweet Polly and George on their special, sweet day that begins their sweet life together. No room for 'bitter' here today. She stamped on the fallen berries and pulled the door open.

"Will you remain with each other until you are parted in death and taken to the Lord?" Deacon Frantz asked Polly and George as they neared the end of the hours-long service and the beginning of their lives together.

"We will," they answered in unison.

The subtle undercurrent of anxiety often shared by most wedding couples had no part in the utter exuberance and love that passed between Polly and George during the ceremony. The glowing faces of the congregation of family and friends, even the notoriously somber members, reflected the complete joy of this couple's union.

Susan sat in her usual place between Rebecca and Cate on the hard wooden bench behind her mother and Elizabeth who held Nan. As the bride's family members, they were assigned the first two rows, much closer to the front than at regular Sunday Meetings.

Despite the importance of the moment, Susan struggled to stay focused. Time had lost all perspective. Her mind was reeling. Events were twisted together as tightly as flax fibers on a spinning wheel. As hard as she tried, while the sacred vows were spoken, she couldn't block the other intrusive images from her thoughts. She saw visions of Samuel and Sarah, just a year earlier, making the same promises as Polly and George, though Sarah now cradled her baby just a few feet away. She pictured Polly's *kist* wedged into the eaves of the loft of their old cabin, though it now waited for Polly at her own house. She envisioned Edward Lehman with his stocky shoulders – my how she had liked him – seated across the center aisle at Samuel's wedding, though Henry Reighart with his lankier frame now sat in his space.

Beside her, Rebecca's tearful eyes glistened just as they had a year ago, but her sister's tears didn't annoy her today as they had then.

It's all happening so fast. So much change – too much change. I can't keep up, she fretted. A lone teardrop escaped the corner of *her* eye, as she felt Rebecca's hand cover hers.

"*Alles ist gut, Schwester*," Rebecca whispered. "Sometimes tears have a mind of their own."

The dust from the last guest's departing wagon had long since settled as Susan lifted the final clean crockery bowl to its place on the summer kitchen shelf. "There," she announced. "*Fertig*! Finally done."

Sarah sat with her infant next to the smoldering hearth. As she nursed Daniel, the babe wrapped four of his tiny fingers around two of hers. "'Twas a fine wedding," she sighed. "Might be a few years 'til the next, but some early sparks were certainly in the air today. John's eyes just light up when he looks at Ruthie Knepper," she added with a hint of mischief.

"And he looks at her every time he's able," Rebecca added building on Sarah's suggestion.

"Now girls," Catherine chided. "John is only 16, not *near* marrying age."

"That may be so, but he's right *at* 'thinking-about-marrying' age," said Sarah.

"I even saw *Jacob* craning to catch a glimpse of Ruthie's younger sister Hannah when he should have been keeping his mind on heaving rocks with the older boys," laughed Rebecca.

"That's enough!" snapped Catherine. "My children are leaving me too quickly as it is. You don't need to be pushing them out of the nest even faster." She moved closer to Sarah who had shifted the baby to her shoulder. "Now hand me my grandson for burping, Sarah. With you and Samuel leaving tomorrow, this could be my last chance for months."

She took the infant gently and held him to her chest adjusting his soft blankets as she headed toward the door. "I'm taking this little one into the house before the night air gets too heavy for him. This may be a summer kitchen, but it's much too wintery in here for my little angel." She looked at Susan before closing the door firmly behind her. "Don't forget to bank the hearth in here before you close up for the night."

"I didn't mean to upset her," said Sarah.

"It's not your fault," Susan said working the coals and ashes of the fire. "I think weddings make everyone think about who they might be paired with someday, even if 'someday' is years away." *Like Henry Reighart*, she thought smiling. "And our family's just had two weddings in one year."

Elizabeth, who had been sitting in the corner quietly knitting, moved toward the door. "It's time passing that's upset Mama. Baby Daniel probably reminds her of her own babies now grown, and Samuel and Polly have started the parade of her children who have grown up overnight into lives of their own. Each one is a passing that must bring pain as well as peace."

"I can't imagine ever parting with my baby. As soon as he's out of sight I miss him. I should have thought before I spoke," Sarah said.

"Best we get to the parlor soon. Don't want to keep Papa waiting for devotions. A day as overflowing with emotion as today needs powerful prayer. God keep us all," said Elizabeth pulling the door open and leaving.

"I'll blow out the lights," Susan said. Now alone, she glanced at the tranquil scene. The orange coals glowing in the hearth reminded her of the berries she had held that morning.

"Bittersweet," she said. "So bittersweet."

-16-

News from Town and Country

George pushed his chair back from the table, belched and smiled at Polly. "That fried sausage and milk gravy was the best I've ever eaten," he said crossing his hands over his stomach. "And the hot cabbage slaw filled every last inch of my belly."

Polly beamed at the compliment. "This December is the coldest I can remember. I'm surprised you can still feel your fingers after working on that framing for Amos Hess's new stable. With all of your hard work *outside*, the least I can do is warm up your *insides*," Polly said throwing off his praise but still showing a slight blush of pride. "I was a little late getting started in the kitchen today. Corn mush from breakfast just didn't sit right on my stomach again."

George moved behind her chair and put his hands on her shoulders. "Glad to see you were able to take *ein ganzes Mahl* this time." He kissed the top of her bonnet. "When you're eating for two, it's best that neither one of you get hungry."

She tipped her head pressing her cheek to his hand. "In that case, if we have a son as *stramm* as his papa, I'll get naught done but eating."

He drew her chair back from the table, stepped in front of her and took her hands to pull her up to his embrace. "And if we have a daughter as *schön* as her mama, I'll get nothing done for looking at her."

She returned the hug and lingered a second before pushing him away playfully. "I've got dishes to clean and racks of candles to dip before getting some more of that wool spun for knitting. Now get yourself back over to Amos's before they come looking for you." She took his hat from the peg by the door and plopped it on his head, then wrapped the bulky woolen scarf around his neck. "Now remember. Not a word to anyone until we're sure. No sense getting anyone else's hopes as high as ours if this little one I think is coming is just our prayers getting ahead of us."

"I know. It's got to be our secret until Christmas Eve at your parents' house." He pulled on his winter coat and laid his hand softly on her stomach. "*Mit Gottes Willen.*"

"It would be a wonderful *Süßigkeit* to offer at the end of the feast that night – just like Sarah's 'sweet' last Christmas," Polly said.

December days faded one into another as Christmas grew near. Evenings came early and lingered like a purring cat. As the family burrowed in against the cold, needles pierced cloth, spinning wheels hummed, pens scratched stiff paper, pages turned and burning logs snapped until eyelids drooped demanding sleep.

Susan sat in the quiet dining room looping the nubby wool yarn repeatedly over her needles as they clicked off the stitches of a scarf she was knitting to donate to the poorhouse in town. The heat of the hearth warmed the soles of her feet as she glanced into the winter kitchen where Cate was flattening a ball of salt dough with Mama's rolling pin. A saucer of seeds and string sat on the floured work table. They would add details to the shapes she would cut and string for Christmas ornaments that would hang on the fragrant fir tree Jacob had installed in the parlor just the day before.

Catherine finished banking the kitchen fire and paused behind Cate. "That dove looks so real I can almost hear it cooing," she commented.

Cate grinned. "Thank you, Mama. I'm going to make one for Polly's new house, too. If they don't have a *Tannenbaum* like we do, she can prop it on their mantle."

"I'm sure she'll love it. You can give it to her when they join us Christmas Eve. It's only two more weeks, you know."

The familiar scents of the Christmas Eve feast filled the house to the very eaves, hovering there long after the last dish was dried and the final preparations were made for the prayerful day to come. After the excitement, the holiday treats and the joyful devotions, sleep had come easily to Susan, but some sixth sense aroused her in the dark morning hours just past midnight. The familiar warmth of Rebecca sleeping beside her was gone, the featherbed turned back and the space vacant. *Rebecca? Where is she?* Susan wondered. Cate's deep breathing from her nearby pallet confirmed her presence, but Rebecca wasn't there.

Susan slipped out of bed taking care not to disturb Cate and went in search of her sister. The upstairs hall was empty, but as Susan stepped delicately down the stairs and made the turn at the landing, she spied Rebecca seated on the bottom step staring into the parlor. Susan sat down silently next to her and together they pondered the silhouetted shapes against the backdrop of the faint glow of the hearth.

"My mind just wouldn't be still," Rebecca finally explained. "The *Tannenbaum*, the meal, the new house, the Christmas devotions are wonderful, just like last year. Even Polly's news about the new baby is such a blessing, but it makes me miss Samuel and his family even more." She turned to Susan. "Changes are swirling around like snowflakes in a whirlwind. They're beautiful, but cold. Sometimes good and bad are all whooshed together. It makes me dizzy."

"I know how you feel, Rebecca. The days creep along from dawn to dusk, but other things are moving too fast to keep up. It doesn't make sense sometimes," Susan said. "But worrying makes me feel even worse and doesn't fix anything."

"So what do you do?" asked Rebecca.

"I try to push the worry out of my brain with happier thoughts," Susan explained. "For instance, when I see how unhappy the war makes John, I try to picture how Ruthie makes him smile. Or when I miss baby Daniel's pink cheeks, I try to imagine how adorable Polly and George's baby will be – probably with enough red, curly hair for three babies."

"And probably enough spirit and sass to keep everybody jumping," Rebecca added with a grin. "Even Polly."

"And we'll be able to see them every Sunday Meeting, at least," Susan said. "And speaking of Sunday Meeting, we've got a full day of prayers ahead of us in just a few hours. We'd better get some sleep before the sun comes up."

"I hate January," sighed Rebecca as she came through the back door with Susan and Cate. "It's the bleakest month of the year. Even Schoolmaster McKeon's frowns look bright in comparison."

"Now, Rebecca," said Catherine wiping her hands on her apron. "I'll stand no disrespect for your schoolmaster. I'm sure he doesn't see many happy faces from the students either."

"If it weren't for school, the days would be twice as long," said Susan hanging her woolen cape by the door. "Our minds can be busy even if our bodies can't. The poem the teacher read by Anne Bradstreet today was *so gut* that I hope some of her verse will be our memory work this week. I already remember two lines. '. . . If winter come, and greenness then do fade, A spring returns, and they more youthful made . . .'

"That surely is a comfort on a dreary winter day like this," Catherine agreed.

"I like figuring numbers," said Cate sitting cross-legged on the rug by the hearth beside Mukki. "Numbers make more sense to me than words, especially the long ones. I don't mind memorizing the times tables, but spelling and verses give me fits."

Catherine planted her hands on her hips. "Well, enough about school and more about supper for now. The menfolk will have 'fits' if things aren't ready for them when they get home.

They've been cutting ice for the Reigharts today, so they'll be past hungry and ready for some hot food and cider. Get to your chores so. . ."

A sharp knocking on the front door stopped Catherine's instructions. "I'll answer the door. You all know what to do."

"*Guten Tag*," said Catherine opening the heavy front door just enough to address the caller.

"*Frau* Royer?" inquired the shivering man with a leather sack slung across his shoulder.

"*Ja,*" Catherine replied.

"I've a packet and two letters for you from the northern county post rider." He handed her the delivery as she opened the door further. "I surely don't envy him such a trip in this weather."

"*Danke.* Step inside and warm yourself a minute, sir, while I gather the payment I owe you," said Catherine moving aside.

"Oh, I'll not soil such fine carpet," said the messenger as he looked past her at the finely appointed hallway, "but I would take some of your hospitality around back, if you don't mind."

"It would be my pleasure," she said. "I'll meet you there." She shut the heavy door and placed the bundle for Daniel on the hall table. *Business figures and reports from the forge no doubt,* she thought. The letters – one for John and one for her – she slid into her apron pocket.

"Thank you for the hot cider and apple butter bread, *Frau* Royer," said the lean young man seated at the winter kitchen work table. His face was leathered for one so young and his pants were splattered with trail mud, though he had pounded his boots vigorously before entering the house.

"Nineteen cents is little payment for bringing a ray of sunshine on a winter day," she answered. "Post riding is a hard profession, but one that rewards you with many smiles, I suppose."

"My territory only reaches Carlisle to the north. Those riders who cover the mountains of Huntingdon County make my job look easy, though it doesn't feel so today, I admit." He washed the last bite of bread down his throat with what remained of his drink. "I noticed your delivery came all the way from Cove Forge – that's quite a journey."

"Yes," she sighed. "Too far away for a son and his family. Bless you for bringing us news."

"And bless you for your kindness," he said. "I'd best be going now. I'll be staying in Waynesburg tonight. Want to settle in before the sun sets."

The post rider had no more than closed the door behind him when the girls clamored around their mother. "Read it, Mama. Hurry! It's from Samuel and Sarah, isn't it? Read it to us. Please!"

She patted her pocket. "After supper when we can take proper time to appreciate it. I saw Papa and your brothers coming down the back lane as the post rider left. They'll be at the table waiting as soon as they've stabled the horses. We have work to do. *Mach schnell.*" She made no mention of the letter for John. *More of that later,* she thought. *He'll want to read it on his own.*

"If you don't take time to chew your food, you'll choke and *never* get to hear what Samuel and Sarah have to say in their letter," Rebecca warned Cate who had stuffed her cheeks with food like a starving chipmunk. "Besides, we need to wait for everyone else to finish, too."

"And clean up as well," added Catherine with a serious but teasing expression. "When we're all seated for devotions, with Papa's permission, I'll read it to everyone." *That is if I can stand to wait that long myself,* she thought.

As the family gathered in the parlor that evening, Daniel deferred to Catherine as she read to the eager listeners.

Liebe Familie,

. . . Samuel's uncle has been very generous in his love and support here in Cove Forge. We could hope for none better, but we miss the familiar faces of our families, especially on special days. Baby Daniel is thriving. His smiles and coos light up a room. When Samuel is exhausted after his labors at the forge, he loves nothing better than to coax reactions from his son. He is determined that 'Papa' will be his first word and repeats it to him over and over . . . You are in our thoughts and prayers.

Alles Liebe

Sarah

Catherine folded the letter in her lap and sighed. Her eyes glazed over, but her posture remained erect and strong. No one spoke as they absorbed the phrases and details of their brother and his family's life so far away. To say more might diminish the impact of the words, throw a shadow over them.

Finally Daniel announced, "A fine letter indeed. Would appear that all's well with them. They'll be especially close to us in our prayers tonight." He paused a moment, then opened the *Bible* on his lap to the *Deuteronomy 32:10* and began, *"He found him in the howling wilderness: he led him about, he instructed him . . ."*

Catherine added a silent prayer. *God, protect my children in the wilderness of Cove Forge*

-17-

Fraying Threads

From the wooden roofing sheets atop Amos Hess's new stable George had a bird's-eye view of the post rider pushing his horse at a furious gallop into town. As the messenger sped through the square and up Main Street, each group he passed erupted in cheers.

Dare I hope? Can it be? George thought. Anxious to be right but reluctant to have his hopes dashed, he strained his ears as the rider passed below him.

"The Redcoats surrender. We've beat the British again!" shouted the ecstatic rider leaning forward well over his horse's mane. "The Redcoats surrender. We've beat those bloody British again." He galloped on into the distance repeating the same glorious refrain.

George let out a whoop to the clouds as he scrambled down the rafters faster than a flea on a hot skillet and ran toward home. "Polly! Polly!" he shouted, knowing she couldn't hear, but unable to help himself. As he rounded the corner, he saw her on the front porch waving her hands over her head and dancing in circles. *She already knows,* he thought. "Polly!" he yelled at the top of his lungs. When she turned to see him, he smiled and began waving his hands and dancing just like her. She laughed as he left a trail of dust behind him in his haste to hug her.

An hour earlier John had arrived in Waynesburg to deliver some herbs and salt from his mother to Polly. He had then made his way to the dry goods store for provisions for the farmstead and waved up to George who was hammering away from his stable perch. John hadn't relished going into town since Isaac Hughes humiliated him in front of the militia recruiter, but the opportunity to see Polly, Sarah and baby Daniel and to garner any news of the war had tempted him to make the trip.

He had just packed his saddlebags with his purchases when the post rider swept through town. His shock matched that of the others who heard the news. Like them, he knew the latest accounts of the war were very encouraging, but British surrender had remained a distant hope. He heard George calling for Polly and the roar of the crowds pouring from the buildings and side streets to cheer. The excitement was contagious, intoxicating, but John mounted his horse and headed in the other direction – out of town.

As he passed the tollgate house at the eastern town limit, he shook his head in disbelief. *Never in a thousand years did I expect news like this. Just two days ago we heard that General Jackson beat them to their knees in New Orleans, and now, this quickly, we've won. It's over.*

It's over. The war's over. The words rang again and again in John's mind as he spurred Tillie toward home. *It's over.* Despite the triumph that the news brought to his heart and the relief of knowing that the pain and suffering and uncertainty for the country were past, he couldn't stay in town and be a part of the celebration. His self-recrimination and sense of alienation made him an outsider to their jubilation. *I should've fought with them – those brave men. I just wasn't strong enough to join –to break with Papa and do what I knew I should do.* His regret left room for little else. The war had ended, but John's confusion and frustration remained.

Elizabeth smoothed the blanket on the bed that she now shared with Cate instead of Polly. *Just one of so many changes*, she thought. "*Frau* Schmucker," she said as she straightened the pillows at the head of the bed. "A wife. My dear Polly is now a wife and soon a mother." She glanced at the far wall where the crib that Nan would soon outgrow stood. "And Samuel is now *Herr* Royer, a husband with a son and soon an ironmaster in his own right." She sighed. "And what of Elizabeth, *mein Gott*? What of me?"

She shook off the question and moved on to her next chore in the boys' front bedroom. As she stooped to clean the small hearth, she caught sight through the frosty window of John riding in the front lane. "Even John and Ruthie exchange smiles. Who knows where that may go, but . . ." Her eyes continued past the lane to the northern horizon peeking through the stark bare branches – toward Mont Alto. *Snow Hill.* She smiled recalling fondly the sublime singing she had heard coming from the solitary red brick cloister she had passed on a trip to Quincy.

Snow Hill, or 'The Nunnery,' as it was called by outsiders, was a religious community that celebrated the Sabbath on Saturday. Though similar to the Dunkards in their beliefs, Snow Hill was home to celibate men and women and a few families that lived harmoniously.

The religious order at Snow Hill had been part of the county for more than 50 years. Believers participated quietly in this offshoot of the Ephrata Cloister – many days travel to the east. The community produced not only farm goods, but its members also illuminated manuscripts and continued a tradition of beautiful choral singing that accentuated women's voices.

Momentarily lost in her daydream, her focus on the present returned when she caught a faint reflection of herself in the windowpane. Where she had been imagining the far buildings of the religious cloister, she now saw her face. Her staring eyes – her view of 'Elizabeth' – hypnotized her. "*Mein Gott*, she whispered. "Is this Your answer? Snow Hill? I wonder what life is like there."

Elizabeth remembered vividly her sense of peace as their wagon had passed by. *Could this have been the Lord speaking to me even then?*

The revelation stunned her, as she dropped into a nearby chair.

"Oh, Elizabeth." John faltered, startled by her presence when he came into his room. "What are you doing here? I mean," he amended suddenly aware of his accusatory tone, "are you all right?"

Standing and adjusting her apron she explained, "Just lost in thought. Keeping up with the world is challenging at times." Then she picked up the bucket of fireplace ashes and returned his look of curiosity. "And what brings you up here this time of the day?"

"I guess you could say the 'challenges' of the world brought us both here," he said taking a seat at David's small desk. "Actually, I have wonderful news from town – a peace treaty has been signed. The war's over – we've won."

Elizabeth took a step toward him. "What wonderful news. But why are you troubled?"

John looked at her and considered. *Should I tell her – show her the letter? I suppose I should show someone – talk to someone.*

He walked over to the window. "Our victory doesn't trouble me. The end of the fighting and suffering doesn't trouble me. How could it?" He paused, then turned to face her. "Elizabeth, it's my heart that troubles me. I struggle every day for peace between my heart and my mind, for peace with Papa, for peace with my faith. I want to find it here, with my family, with . . . with Ruthie. But I need to participate, to contribute . . . to belong."

"I pray every day for your struggle, John," she said touching his cheek. "We've all felt your pain."

He walked around her to the small dresser and opened the middle drawer. Reaching under the folded clothing, he pulled out the letter his mother had given him the day before. "Samuel's written to me." He handed her the folded sheets. "He's invited me to live with them at Cove Forge." Elizabeth's eyes widened. "He says there's more tolerance for troubled souls – more acceptance of different views of God and the world. He thinks I could be happier there."

He waited as she read the lines, folded the pages and returned them. "You must do what feeds your spirit, John. As much as I'd miss you, I'd never deny you that peace."

"But how can I leave? I wait every day for some sign, some confirmation of what to do." He turned to the window facing the creek. "As much as Papa needs my help with the farm and everything else, I feel his disappointment every time he looks at me.

He's always yelling at me. It's getting harder and harder to 'Honor my father.'" Returning the letter to the dresser, he began to pace. "This awful winter gives me too much time to think. When I'm working – at the sawmill or harvesting ice – I can stand it, but the days are too short and the nights too long to give me any peace."

He took Elizabeth's hands. "Don't tell anyone about the letter, *Schwester*. Only Mama and you can know until I can get myself straight."

She squeezed his hands. "I'll say nothing, *Bruder*. Except to God."

-18-

Tinkers and Snakes

L ine after line of thick, bristly rope stretched between the trees and eaves of buildings all around the Royer home, as familiar a sign of spring as the yellow-green buds on branches and the early golden dandelion blooms. Elizabeth and Susan made their way from the back of the house toward an expanse of line strung from the front corner of the summer kitchen roof to the tall oak. Their arms were supporting opposite ends of the heavy, six-foot roll of prized wool carpet from the parlor.

"I think I'd rather manage a plow than spring houseclean," grunted Susan. "Especially with so many rugs and curtains to beat clean and air out."

"It's a chore, I know, but isn't it nice to chase away winter and feel the fresh air fill the house again?" said Elizabeth not expecting her younger sister to agree.

Jacob passed by the girls on his way to the barn. "Watch out for snakes today," he warned. "I just chased the rats out of the icehouse and I scared up a couple of snakes, too. They won't stay there long without any more vermin to eat. Hard to tell where they might show up."

Susan cringed. "I hate snakes." She stopped in her tracks long enough to throw a glance at the foundation of the summer kitchen.

"Well, they probably don't much care for you either," he teased. "See you at noon meal."

"Keep moving, Susan," said Elizabeth. "This is heavy."

They shuffled along again, each wrestling with their end of the rug, until they reached the ten-foot length of rope. As they inched toward the center of the carpet roll, they adjusted their handholds. When they were three feet from each other, they both turned to face the line six feet above the ground. "Are you ready?" asked Susan.

"*Ja*," said Elizabeth.

"On three," Susan directed. "*Eins – Zwei – Drei.*" Together they heaved the wool carpet coil midway over the rope and proceeded to unroll it to its full eight-foot length. Elizabeth dug into her apron pocket for the large wooden pins to secure it as Susan headed to the summer kitchen for the rug beaters.

From the corner of her eye she spied movement on the distant dirt path leading to the house. "The tinker's wagon's coming up the front lane," she shouted toward the open door of the dining room. "I'll fetch the broken pots and pans."

Cate stuck her head out the door and watched the small covered wagon jangling with all sorts of paraphernalia pull to a stop. A lanky, tweed-capped man hopped down and tied his swaybacked mule to the front hitching  post. "I'll tell Mama he's here and to get the dull knives," squealed Cate as she disappeared into the house.

Before the tinker made it halfway up the stone walk to the front door, Catherine stepped off the porch to greet him. At her approach, the man snatched the wool cap from his head and made a deep bow revealing a mass of tight red curls. "Top 'o the mornin', Ma'am," he said in his Irish brogue. "I hope I'm not disturbin' you this fine day."

Catherine wiped her hands on her apron. "Your timing is *perfekt*. We're chasing away the winter dirt and stink today. Couldn't be a better time for mending our pots and tinware to match a clean-swept house."

"And sharpenin' your knives to help cook all the delicious meals I've heard tell of?" he hinted.

"That, too." She smiled and cocked her head. "You can set up your welding and your grinding wheel in the back – *and* have yourself some dinner in the summer kitchen when it suits."

"T'would be a pleasure, Ma'am," he said bowing again as he backed away. "And feel free to have a look round me wagon. Got some dandy things there that might just tickle your fancy."

"You just mind your mending, young man. *I'll* be minding my 'fancy.'" Catherine started into the house, but then hesitated and turned back. "*And* my daughters," she added with a warning scowl. *Especially Fräulein Rebecca,* she thought. *She'd be hanging on every word of his news and gossip. Better to have Elizabeth serve the summer kitchen meals to the workers today and keep Rebecca scrubbing floors in the house. Little pitchers have big ears,* she thought making her way back inside to continue her supervision and labor.

Fragments of doughy, chicken-sopped noodles clinging to the sides of the two large pans were all that remained of the *Bott Boi,* the noon meal's hearty main dish. The molasses cake had been reduced to a scattering of crumbs. The bit of stewed rhubarb and buttered squash that remained in the serving bowls would accompany the evening's salt pork and mush.

The business of eating had ended, but the calm before the next 'storm' of activity hung over everyone at the dining room table. Even Nan was nodding off early for her afternoon nap. The grating of the tinker's sharpening edged into the hovering silence.

"Has everyone kept clear of his wagon?" Daniel grumbled. "Not a thing there that we need or that I'll give good money for." He glanced at John. "And I'll burn any newspapers he tries to peddle."

John stared at his dirty plate. *Just leave it alone.* He poked at a bit of chicken bone. *I need to get out of here.* "Lots of plowing to finish. *Kann ich gehen?*" he asked Daniel.

"*Und ich?*" added Jacob, sensing the tension and anxious to support John.

Daniel stood. "You're *all* excused. Back to work. *Schnell!*"

Everyone at the table rose as directed and headed to their various tasks. As John reached for his hat by the door, Daniel pushed deliberately in front of him to be the first to leave. John gave way to his father's show of authority, but anger tightened across his shoulders. Jacob leaned in to retrieve his hat and whispered to John, "Peace, *Bruder.*"

Oblivious to the silent conflict, Cate dashed out the door behind her father. "I'll be back as soon as I get my doll. I think I left it by the milk house when I went for the butter."

"Hurry," Catherine shouted after her. She picked up Nan for her nap and taking note of the nervous halt in activity she said, "You heard your father. Back to work."

"Good afternoon, Mr. Royer," said the tinker looking up from his grinding wheel as Daniel stomped past eyeing him suspiciously. Daniel only grunted and then looked with equal disdain at the tinker's wagon parked nearby.

John followed not far behind. He paused by the tinker and answered respectfully *for* his father, "Good afternoon, Ian." *If Papa only knew how many times you've delivered newspapers to me, he'd have your head*, he thought.

They shared a complicit smile.

"What's this?" Daniel yelled. Reaching under the bench of the tinker's wagon, he yanked out a folded broadsheet and waved it viciously in the air. "More blasphemy!" He stormed toward Ian. "I forbid such rubbish on my property." He ripped the page in half, threw the pieces on the ground and continued toward the tinker.

Ian abandoned his grinding wheel and stumbled backwards in retreat. John stepped in front of his father meeting him chest to chest. Daniel tried to shove him aside, but John stood firm.

"Leave him alone, *Vater*," said John. "He has no quarrel with you."

Daniel glared at his son. "You dare defy me?" They stood nose to nose. "Step aside," he growled low and hard. But John held his ground.

Behind them Jacob helped the tinker to his feet and led him in a wide circle away from the heated encounter. "*Geh,*" Jacob whispered. "Get your due from my mother at the house and leave. I'll bring your equipment to the end of the lane directly. This is family business – not any of your doing."

"Much obliged," said the tinker. He took off at a run.

212

"I said 'make way' and I'll not say it again," Daniel ordered. He huffed as he pushed John's shoulder further aside only to discover the tinker had gone and Jacob stood in his place. "Gone," Daniel scoffed. "Run off like a scared rabbit. To the Devil with him." Then he spun around. "As for you . . ." He marched toward John. "You will *not* preach to me – not *ever* again."

John's chest rose and fell. He pressed his clenched fists tightly against his thighs. "No, *you're* the preacher, *Vater. You* judge and condemn. I can never match *your* preaching."

"It will be *Gott* who judges you. Not me – *Gott*." Daniel pointed toward the sky.

"And what about *you*?" John countered taking a step closer to him. "Will God judge *you*? Will he condemn your *hypocrisy*?"

"*My* hypocrisy? With your unclean soul, your unbaptized spirit, you dare to speak of *my* hypocrisy?" He drew back his arm and dove at John, but teetered backward fuming as Jacob grabbed his elbow. Daniel shook Jacob off and bent over grabbing his knees and drawing long, deep breaths to regain control.

John kept his distance, but would not be silent. "Wasn't it hypocrisy to rail against the war while you reaped the harvest of its destruction – while you filled your pockets at the price of men's lives who fought to protect you and your family?"

"Silence!" Daniel seethed. "I did my part." He stood erect. "I've always done my part."

"And judged yourself worthy," John added.

Every muscle in Daniel's broad, powerful body quivered.

John threw his arms to the sky surrendering to the moment – letting fly words he had swallowed for so long. "The troops at Valley Forge – the sacrifice you made for George Washington and his men. If not for Opa Royer, you would've charged a penny a pound profit for those cattle and then offered a prayer of Thanksgiving. Yet you praise yourself and condemn me."

Jacob stood at the ready praying the worst had passed, but knowing it hadn't.

"Out of my sight you Godless, ungrateful wretch." Daniel glared at John. "*Geh mir aus den Augen!* I can't bear the sight of you!" he bellowed.

The second that Daniel's thundering faded, a chilling, high-pitched shriek of pain filled the air silencing all else. Everyone froze, dumbstruck.

The source of the cry was immediately apparent as Cate stumbled out screaming from behind the milk house a few yards to John's left. Her little face was pale and tight with fear, her eyes frozen like dark river stones. She clutched her hand in front of her staring at it as if it belonged to someone else.

John gathered her into his arms as Daniel and Jacob came running. "Snakebite!" John shouted to them over Cate's wailing. He stared at the two puncture marks in the already red, swollen

skin just above the wrist of her small trembling hand. He hugged her and rocked soothingly. "Shhh, Cate, shhh. It'll be all right."

"Get her to the house," Daniel ordered stooping beside them. "Jacob, tell Mama to get the ammonia. I'll get some gunpowder for a poultice. Run!"

John clutched Cate to his chest and ran toward the house.

"Mama! Mama!" Cate sobbed. "It hurts. Make it stop hurting, Mama."

Catherine and the other girls met Jacob halfway to the door. "What's happened?" she pleaded. "Where's my Cate? She's screaming – I hear her screaming!"

"Snakebite, Mama. John's got her," Jacob explained. "Papa says to get the ammonia. He's gone to get the gunpowder."

"*Gott im Himmel, mein Liebchen!*" Catherine cried. "Susan, bring the ammonia to the parlor and spread a blanket." The frantic mother ran to meet John. "*Mein Liebchen, mein armes Liebchen.*" She stroked Cate's head as she walked alongside John carrying his fragile bundle.

After more than 24 hours by Cate's side, Catherine had finally succumbed to sleep. No one else would presume to nurse Cate – the bond was a lifeline for both mother and child. The doctor could do no more than their home remedies.

Catherine curled into the nest of her skirts on the hardwood floor of the parlor. Her head rested on the edge of the settee covered by the featherbed where her suffering child lay sleeping. Cate's tiny enflamed fingers protruded from the linen bandages that secured the poultice. The limb had swollen so grossly that the skin across the knuckles had split open, the cold compress tinged pink with blood. The vomiting had continued for hours, long after her wracked body had nothing else to give up. Exhaustion finally allowed the girl to sleep in spite of the throbbing pain.

Elizabeth, draped in a nearby wing chair, had also stood a constant prayerful vigil. Daniel was at the table in his office, his head collapsed on top of his dirt-streaked arms.

Susan placed a large tureen of chicken stew on the dining room table as she balanced a squirming Nan on her hip. She had skimmed some of the nutritious broth hoping that Cate would eventually be able to keep a bit down. "Call everyone to the table," she said to Rebecca who had a basket of biscuits in hand. "They've got to keep up their strength. But don't wake Mama if she's sleeping. We can take her something to eat later."

At the mention of 'Mama,' Nan whimpered. "I want Mama. Where's Mama?"

"Be still," said Susan bouncing the toddler. "Mama needs to be with Cate 'til she gets better. *Pray God she does get better,* she thought.

Daniel's shoulders sagged as he stood at the head of the dining room table. David, to his right, had assumed all of his father's duties in the crisis. Elizabeth, Susan, Rebecca, and Nan stood in a line along the opposite side of the table. Jacob came in from the side door and took his usual place leaving a space for John between himself and David. An uneasy silence followed as the group awaited John's arrival so Daniel could offer the blessing.

Daniel stared at the empty space and everyone else stared at the bowls in front of them.

"He's not coming, *Vater*," David said. "Best he stays wherever he is, as I see it."

"Be quiet. *Schweige bitte*, David," snapped Rebecca frowning hard at him "You're so nasty sometimes. *Sei nicht so gemein.* We all belong together now. John belongs here with us."

"Enough," Daniel barked. "We'll say the blessing."

Before Daniel could begin the prayer, Jacob bolted from the table and out the door. All eyes jumped to Daniel. No one spoke. Daniel paused, looked blankly at the open door, then bowed his head and clasped his hands in front of him, a signal for all to do the same. "*Gnädiger Gott im Himmel . . .*"

The basket of biscuits rounded the table only once before Susan left as well, in search of her brothers. As with Jacob's leave-taking, her departure prompted no comment from Daniel who was drained of any desire for more conflict. He had 'lost' one son already and might well lose a daughter. He had energy for little else.

The stream has always soothed Jacob – the turning of the mill wheel and stones, thought Susan as she considered where she might discover one of her brothers. Making her way around the side of the smokehouse, she spied Jacob's stocky frame seated beside a towering oak and staring upstream at the gristmill. She lowered herself next to him, but said nothing.

"I should have waited," he finally said slowly.

"Waited?" Susan was confused. "For what? When?"

"The rats. If I'd only waited until evening like I should've – like John told me – the snakes would've stayed at the icehouse until we were all safely in for the night. But I was too anxious to finish my chores – too . . ." His speech stumbled. "Too impatient to wait, and now . . . now Cate might . . . she might . . ."

"You're not to blame, Jacob." Susan laid her hand on his shoulder. He dropped his head and turned away. "It's no one's fault, not even that nasty snake's." She shuddered. "I know I said 'I hate snakes,' but that's not really fair. The creature was just defending himself, doing what God gave snakes the ability to do." She rubbed his back. "Sometimes terrible things just happen. We have to try hard not to ask 'why,' and just pray for the strength to get through." She sat quietly respecting Jacob's need to collect himself, to move forward.

As they lingered side by side, the sunlight filtering through the tender foliage overhead speckled the ground. Scattered chirps and the bubbling creek competed with the silence. Jacob sighed heavily twice before he finally stood.

"Well," he said with a new, albeit tenuous, resolve. "The farm isn't going to run itself. Time to stop brooding and get to work." He looked down at Susan with a smile of his own and offered her a hand. Together they surveyed the scene before them. "*Danke,* Susan. *Du bist meine kluge kleine Schwester.* You're wiser than you know. I'm glad God gave you the ability to talk good sense to a foolish brother when he needs it."

-19-

Too Many Farewells

A week after Cate was well enough to chase Nan around the summer kitchen and to reclaim her chore of gathering eggs, John would leave the Royer farmstead. Cate's recovery was the sign he was seeking – the clear indication that he should move away. The dreadful argument between him and his father had caused Cate to hide beside the milk house where the rattler bit her. As he carried her to the house that day, he promised God that if Cate lived, he would leave. Each day he remained at home brought little but misery for everyone he loved and himself. He had stayed on through spring planting, the toughest part of the year, when responsibilities would have fallen most heavily on Jacob in his absence.

On the day he had determined to go, John took his place at the table and drank in the usual early morning scene. *Wish I could hold it in my head – this place – this family. But . . .* He looked down at his bowl.

David, surly as ever, had finished his corn mush and bacon and left the breakfast table for the tannery. The girls and Catherine busied themselves with the usual morning routine. As Daniel finished his cider, Jacob scraped his bowl for the last spoonful of his morning meal. *I'll miss him most of all,* thought John seated across from his younger brother.

John took one long last look at the hearth, the portrait of George Washington above it, his Mama's and sisters' sunbonnets hanging on the wall and Mukki waiting to  accompany the next person out the door. He stood, moved to the door and sighed. "Papa. Mama," he said. "I gathered a few things and saddled Maggie before dawn today. Samuel's written to offer me a place in Cove Forge and I'll be leaving to join him."

Everyone gazed at the somber young man before them. No one spoke. They all understood his choice without asking why, but the shock and sadness of this inevitable moment held them as tightly as flies in a spider's web. One by one the tearful siblings hugged their brother and wished him well. Mama watched the procession and fell in line behind her children, waiting for his embrace. She took his face in her hands and with teary eyes said, "Be safe, my son. This will always be your home. *Bete zu Gott* that you find peace."

Catherine reached into the small pocket on the inside of her waistband and retrieved a loop of rawhide strung with four gold coins, the accumulated savings from years of butter sales. Knowing this day might come, on one of her visits to town she had paid the blacksmith to use his auger to drill small holes in the disks to put on the string for safekeeping. She draped it around John's neck and kissed the top of his head.

"*Danke, Mama*," he whispered with a catch in his voice.

Daniel remained at the table staring at his tankard. "Maggie and the saddle would bring at least 40 dollars at auction," he said without looking at John.

Catherine closed her eyes and shook her head. Jacob grimaced. The rest were simply stunned by his indifference.

John removed his mother's gift of coins and laid it on the table in front of his father. "I'll repay you the rest as soon as I've earned the money at whatever labor I find," John answered.

Daniel nodded. "Best you take the old squirrel gun and a hunting knife from the barn, too," he added. "I can pick them up on my next trip north to the forge."

"*Auf Wiedersehen*, Papa," said John, putting on his hat to leave.

"*Auf Wiedersehen*, John," said Daniel. He downed the last of his drink, planted the mug on the table, picked up the string of coins and walked out of the dining room to his office without looking back.

John's final stop before setting out on his journey was the Kneppers' farm. Ruthie had taken three days to consider John's invitation to accompany him. They were, unarguably, too young for marriage, but Samuel had agreed to find a suitable situation for Ruthie if she wanted to come along and wait until a wedding would become appropriate.

She would stay in Waynesburg, she had decided sadly. It was just too soon for her to make such a weighty choice, though she would miss John terribly. Today would mean not only goodbye for some time to come, but also a reluctant end to thoughts of sharing a future together.

As he rode away from the neat fields and tidy farms on the edge of Waynesburg, John thought, *How can I blame her? To give up her secure home and loving family – for what? A difficult life four mountain ridges away in a smoky settlement of iron forge workers.* He sighed and looked back over his shoulder. *If only I could stay.* "Goodbye, Ruthie."

Life went on at the Royers', though now they had three fewer family members to take their seats at the table and prayers, three less pairs of hands to turn the daily wheels of commerce and of necessity. Adjustment to such loss would take time – and prayer.

Steadily, the tempo of living began to return. The snakebite in April that could easily have taken Cate's young life had, instead, given her an extra measure of vitality even beyond her usual childhood exuberance prior to the attack. Since regaining her health, she had acquired a wealth of enthusiasm that brought a sparkle to her brown eyes and an eagerness to take in all of life she could. No task was so dull, no day so gray that seven-year-old Cate couldn't find some joy in it.

Cate's brush with death had been the Royer's first experience with nearly losing a child. Susan and Rebecca's accident at the kiln the previous year, though potentially life-threatening, had been largely unobserved and quickly resolved with Susan's broken arm the only real casualty. However, the entire family had witnessed Cate's struggle and valiant recovery from the rattler's venom. Catherine had been by her daughter's side to the brink of death and back. The bond they now shared was obvious whenever they were together, whenever they looked at each other.

Susan felt a quiet envy at their connection, but couldn't resent something so touching and rare. She and Rebecca agreed that Cate's delight in the world filled the void in their mother's heart left by the children who no longer slept under her roof, ate her meals or shared their devotions.

Spring's yellow-green grass dried to summer straw.

A sudden cloudburst pelted the tin roof of the summer kitchen as the family gathered for noon meal. The storm washed the hot, hazy July air and soaked the dusty soil giving the valley a reprieve from the oppressive doldrums of midsummer. After the short-lived rain, the men reluctantly returned to the gristmill, tannery and fields. A fresh breeze blowing through the windows helped to lighten the cleanup chores for the girls and their mother.

"I'll have Jacob fetch some ice from the icehouse later. I think we should treat ourselves to some peach iced cream today before Polly goes back to town," Catherine announced as she draped the damp towel over the edge of the basin.

"Sounds wonderful, Mama," said Polly.

"Can we go down to the creek and cool our feet until it's time to help peel the fruit and turn the ice cream crank, Mama?" asked Cate.

"*Das ist eine gute Idee*," Catherine said. "Now scoot, all of you. I'll call when I need you."

The tip of the house roof and some towering oak branches blocked the worst of the sweltering mid-afternoon sun from the creek just below the smokehouse. The six Royer girls gathered in the welcome shade in a rare moment of sweet leisure. Even Elizabeth resting at the base of the tree glanced up from her hymnbook to watch all of her sisters' antics.

A very-pregnant Polly sat arch-backed on a large stone dangling her bare toes in the cool creek water. "I'm glad I  convinced George that I'd be in good hands today if he took that job over in Five Forks. Otherwise, I wouldn't have been able to come to visit. He's been watching me like a mother hen for the last month," she added kicking the water with her toes to splash Cate who was hopscotching from one large streambed stone to another.

"But he's a handsome 'mother hen,'" said Rebecca giggling.

Cate leaned her face toward the spray welcoming the friendly assault. "Now *both* ends of me are cool. Thanks, Polly," she said.

"Look at *my* splash," Nan squealed as she jumped up and down in the water with Rebecca and Susan each holding a hand to balance her.

"What a whirlpool!" Polly said. "I can't believe how fast you're growing."

"I can't think of a better place to be than right here," said Rebecca. "Thank goodness this July has come with more rain than usual. I'd much rather water my feet than the garden."

226

Polly glanced to her right at the top of the creek bank. "Last year the celery in that bare plot was more than *knee* high." She stared down at her apron. "And this year I forget what my *knees* look like. I haven't been able to see them for so long."

"By the looks of it, you should be able to see them pretty soon," Susan teased.

"This baby can't come too soon for me," Polly said wiping her sweaty brow. "I was hoping that the bumpy wagon ride over here might hurry nature along."

"I need hands for peelin' and arms for crankin' before this ice is nothing but a puddle," Catherine called from the top of the rise leading to the house.

"I can bring a tongue for tastin' for sure," said Cate high-stepping her way out of the creek.

"That makes six of us," added Rebecca.

Polly wiggled to the side of her stone perch and eased herself carefully off the edge until she felt the cool, silky grass of the slope.

"Wait, Polly," said Susan spying the strain on her sister's face as she struggled to stand. "I'll help you up." She transferred Nan's hand from her own to Rebecca's free hand and moved toward Polly.

"Don't be silly," scoffed Polly waving Susan off. "I can . . ." But the swing of her arm threw her off balance. As her weight shifted, the ball of her foot pushed against the slippery mud under the grass and slid out from under her. She tried to break her fall, but the huge rock was tight up against her right arm, leaving only her left arm free to cushion the blow as she hit the ground face first.

"Polly!" screamed the girls.

Catherine came running down the hill frantically. "Stay still, Polly. Don't try to get up."

Polly rolled to her back and looked up at the circle of frightened faces above her. In an instant, she started laughing as she pointed at them. "I've never seen so many eyeballs," she teased. "It looks like somebody broke open a bag of marbles."

Catherine and Elizabeth got on either side of her and helped her cautiously to her feet. "Don't laugh," Catherine scolded, wiping mud and grass from Polly's forehead. "You scared the life out of us!"

"You know me, Mama. Anything for a good laugh."

"Well, you're the only one laughing," Catherine said. "Now let's get you to the house and clean you up. George won't trust us ever again if he sees you looking like this. Rebecca, go get some water heating on the stove." She kissed Polly's muddy cheek. "No sweet iced cream until you're scrubbed free of this mud. You look like a gingerbread cookie."

Polly smiled. "Gingerbread is one of George's fav . . . ohh," She stopped short and tightened at the sudden stab of pain.

Catherine stared at her anxiously. "What's wrong, Polly?"

228

Polly tried to stay calm. She drew some deep breaths, paused and smiled. "It's his favorite sw . . ." She suddenly doubled over with an intense moan as Elizabeth and Catherine fought to support her. "Oh, Mama," she wailed. "Mama, what's happening? My baby . . . Mama, my baby!" Another sharp cramp shot through her. "No!" she screamed.

"Polly," Catherine instructed with a forced calm. "We need to get you in the house. Try to keep walking, Polly. Lean on us – we'll make it. Just breathe deep."

Polly nodded as her eyes, wide with panic, pleaded with Catherine. The three began the slow 20-yard walk to the house. "You're a strong girl. You'll have a strong, healthy child." Catherine tried to reassure her terrified daughter. *Gott, hilf uns,* she prayed silently.

"Susan," Catherine called. "Go find David. Tell him to ride Tillie to Five Forks as fast as he can to fetch George."

"Yes, Mama." Susan sped away.

"Here, George," said Rebecca putting a mug of cold cider beside the flickering oil lamp on the summer kitchen table in front of her distraught brother-in-law. George propped his elbows on the table holding his head in his hands oblivious to the offer. Rebecca put her hand on his back. "Mama's delivered lots of babies. She says the first one always seems to take forever."

"But it's been almost ten hours," he moaned. He looked at Rebecca pleading, "I want to see her. I need to see my Polly."

"Mama and Elizabeth and Susan are taking good care of her. They'll send for you as soon as they can," Jacob added from the other side of the room. Cate and Nan slept fitfully on a pad of blankets at his feet.

"We men must keep our distance during the birthing," Daniel said seated at the opposite end of the table. "I've done it more than ten times, but it never gets any easier. The minutes are hours long."

Just then, Susan appeared at the door. At the sight of her ashen, tear-streaked face, everyone's heart stopped. "George," she whispered. "Mama says you're to go to Polly."

George lunged past her at a dead run for the house. Rebecca took hold of Susan's hands. "What is it, Susan?" she asked fearing, as everyone, the worst.

"The baby was breech – not in the right position to be born," she choked. She looked around the room with vacant eyes. "There's nothing that Mama – that anyone – can do." She couldn't say more for crying.

Daniel came to her softly. "Tell us, Susan. Polly? The baby? They're . . ."

"Oh, Papa," she sobbed falling into his arms. "Her baby . . . such a tiny, sweet boy . . . he never drew a breath. And . . . and Polly . . . Polly's so weak." Susan clutched her father's shirt. "Mama can't stop the bleeding." Daniel held her head to his chest. "Papa, she's dying . . . Polly's dying."

Daniel closed his eyes as he breathed deeply. "We must pray," he said finally. "We must pray for the souls of these two dear children of God." He opened his arms inviting his older children into a circle. They staggered to him and bowed their heads as he began, "*Vater unser im Himmel . . .*"

Catherine and her daughters had dressed Polly all in white – the same cape and the apron she had worn on her wedding day less than a year before. The infant completely swaddled in white linen lay in the crook of her arm. The coffin of fresh cut pine stood draped in white in the family parlor. George and the remaining Royers dressed in black met with friends and family who had come to extend their condolences and, if they chose, pull back the linen sheet far enough to view Polly's milk-white face.

George, Polly's parents and her siblings, stunned by a grief still blunted by disbelief, were posed in the line of chairs to receive visitors. Daniel and the boys nodded their heads in response to supportive words, Catherine and the girls wept silently, but George remained unresponsive.

 Two long days and nights George had stayed at Polly's bedside. When life left her, he had wailed and collapsed refusing to release her hand until Elizabeth gently loosened the fingers he had entwined in Polly's cold grip. Since then his brothers had directed his actions as if he were a lifeless marionette. He had eaten nothing, drunk only when urged and said not one word. The only sign of life he offered was to turn the handkerchief embroidered by his beloved over and over in his hands fingering the raised letters "PR" and "GS" that she had stitched in the early days of their romance.

The prayer service at the house and the burial the following day prolonged the aura of unreality. The Royers' world ground to a halt for 72 hours. Brethren from the fellowship stepped in immediately to maintain as best they could the operations of the farmstead and household duties without being too intrusive. Until the final visitors set the house in order and departed, the loss of Polly and her child consumed the family's life. They fell into bed that night knowing that the next morning would challenge their paralysis. They would have to begin to live again
– without Polly.

The next morning's heavy mist dissolved into hot afternoon.

Daniel stared at the accounting summaries from Cove Forge in his office. *Samuel should get the letter about Polly today . . . Why God? Of all my daughters, she had the most spirit, the most strength.* Alone in his office, Daniel sobbed.

Catherine kneaded a mound of dough in the summer kitchen. *After the rye, some pumpernickel . . . pies for Sunday Meeting . . . gather the clothes for Monday washing . . .* Her fist stopped atop the yeasty mound. *Don't think about her.* She slammed the dough onto the floured table raising a white haze and continued kneading. *Hard-boil some eggs . . . tell Rebecca to churn the butter . . . the eggs . . .* "Cate," she shouted. "Cate, come here."

Cate came through the door wary of the tone of her mother's voice. "Yes, Mama," she said.

"Gather the eggs," she said peering vacantly at her daughter. Their eyes met and both acknowledged the pain. Catherine flipped the dough and raised another dusting of flour.

"Looks like a cloud, Mama. Like heaven," said Cate. She hugged her mother quickly. "Polly will surely have the angels laughing by now."

David inspected the scraping tools in the tannery. *Poor George. Better not to love so much and risk so much pain.*

Jacob listened to the huge stones pulverize the grain as he bagged the powdery flour. *Grain to flour. Dust to dust. Her body to the spirit.*

Elizabeth worked the baffles of the butter churn with Nan tight against her. Nan clung to everyone now. Elizabeth frowned. *What did Polly do, Lord, but love the life you gave her? Of all of us, why her?*

Susan and Rebecca placed their sunbonnets over their caps and headed for the four-square garden. "Do you want to have babies some day?" asked Rebecca.

"If God grants them," Susan answered.

"But what if . . ."

"Be quiet," Susan snapped. "Polly never asked 'What if?' She lived life every day as completely as she could. And so should we."

-20-

Weaving a New Tapestry

"Come and get me," teased Nan as she zigged and zagged between the overgrown beds of the four-square garden with 14-month-old Daniel toddling in pursuit. "Peek-a-boo." She poked her head from behind a high mound of fuzzy squash leaves startling him into a fit of high-pitched squeals.

"Samuel couldn't wait until his son could walk," Sarah said to Susan as they watched the antics. "But now we can barely keep up with him. Especially since Jane was born." She glanced toward the summer kitchen as Daniel ducked behind her legs and peeked out at Nan who was now chasing him. "I hope the baby's not too much trouble for your mother and Elizabeth while they're working on the noon meal."

"I'm sure they love her company," Susan reassured Sarah. "Your visit has been powerful medicine for mother – for all of us – since Polly . . ."

The two looked at each other in silent shared mourning. Sarah nodded.

"I can hardly believe you've been here for a week already. The time's passed too quickly," said Susan.

"I know what you mean," Sarah agreed. "I just wish the time would be that swift on the trip *back* to Cove Forge. It takes all of five days with the babies and the wagons, and the way stations can barely accommodate us." She hugged Daniel against her skirt. "I don't mean to complain, but the trip here was easier because I knew all of you and my family were waiting at the end. Going back will feel endless."

Rebecca approached them, her apron laden with three heads of cabbage. "The last of the season," she announced. "More for the sauerkraut crocks." She swung the vegetables gently in her apron hammock and mused, "Polly just hated the smell – more than any of us."

"I remember the funny way she'd crinkle her nose," said Cate as she pulled some cucumbers nearby and added them to her gathering basket. She made the face she remembered at Nan and Daniel who both grinned. "Looks like my basket's full. Let's go see what's happening in the summer kitchen," she said to the tots as she passed the basket to Sarah and took them by the hand. "Noon meal will be ready soon."

The threesome headed for the garden gate.

236

"So many things must remind you of Polly," Sarah said to Susan. "It must be very hard."

"It's getting a little easier. At least we can talk to each other about it now – say her name aloud without crying." Susan pinched the lacy leaves from a small bunch of dusty orange carrots and laid them on top of the cucumbers.

"All of us but George," Rebecca added shaking her head. "He seems more and more lost every day. He sits in their house day after day with the curtains pulled and rocks the empty cradle his father built. He won't allow anyone to touch a thing, hardly eats and refuses to talk, especially to the church deacons or his father. Everyone's worried about him."

Sarah sighed focusing on the stately stone house ahead of them, the site of the tragic loss. "Samuel stopped to visit with George just after we got here – nearly two weeks ago – and invited him to come back to Cove Forge with us, to get a new start. He'd have no trouble finding work. John's not had a day's rest since he arrived. We've been praying every day that George will come."

"Maybe he *should* leave Waynesburg, at least for a time," Susan agreed. "Some place away from so many things that remind him of Polly."

"You're probably both right," Rebecca said, kicking the fuzzy head of a dandelion stalk in her path. "But, I hate to see someone else leaving. Like these seeds in the breeze, just flying away."

Just then the dinner bell rang out from the summer kitchen. "Already?" Sarah sighed. "Each day we're here goes by faster than the last."

Sarah and the two girls gathered up their garden harvest and began their trek toward the house.

"What a glorious day!" said Rebecca scanning the line of resplendent trees along the stream. "The Lord must send these crisp blue skies and rainbow leaves in the fall to give us the extra energy we need for the harvest."

Sarah breathed in a waft of sweet apples and cinnamon that drifted past them and smiled. "Your mother's cooking certainly provides some energy, too." The trio stepped up their pace across the back yard to the waiting feast of food and family.

"It's a sound plan, Papa," said Samuel examining the large sheet of paper unrolled on Daniel's office table. "I can certainly understand the need for an addition to the house with all of the *changes* around here." He suppressed what would have been a large belch. "But I'm thankful that Mama's good cooking hasn't *changed* a bit. That hog maw *hat gut geschmeckt*, but I can hardly move now." He fell against the back of the chair and patted his stomach.

"This harvest was a trial without you and John," said Daniel stroking his graying beard and pacing the floor. "I had to pay out nearly twice the wages for additional workers this year just to clear the crop. It was all Jacob and *Herr* Fahnestock could do to keep up with the mill, and David, even with the help of Sean McBride who's become quite an industrious worker, was pushed to maintain operations at the tannery.

Jacob stood by the office door listening. He felt the rough edges of the new flint stone in his pocket that John had sent to him with Samuel and turned away from his father. *You have only yourself to blame for that, Papa – driving my brother away the way you did.*

"When this grand new kitchen is added directly to the house," said Daniel pointing to the building plan, "Mama and the girls won't have to waste so much energy traipsing to and from the summer kitchen. Plus, I'll have much more room for storage in the old winter kitchen, and in the rooms above the new kitchen I can expand my office space for record keeping.

"Then we can use the summer kitchen as housing for one or two permanent hired help – maybe some indentures from the old country. They're much less costly than seasonal help and more reliable," David added.

"We may even find some girl to help Mama with the household. The house isn't getting any smaller and she's not getting any younger." Daniel rubbed his lower back. "We're both beginning to feel the years."

A knock from outside Daniel's office interrupted the conversation. They shared a curious look as David opened the door to find George's imposing frame. "George," said Daniel, as the other two echoed. "Welcome, son." As George stepped inside, Daniel wrapped a supporting arm around his shoulder. "Sit down and have some cider with us."

"And maybe a slice of Mama's shoo fly pie, too," added Samuel. He immediately noticed the change in George since their meeting weeks earlier. He was standing taller, shoulders drawn back, and his green eyes had a spark of life, however faint.

George removed his hat and held it in front of him. "As tempting as that is, I'm afraid I can't stay that long." He took a step toward Samuel, seated at the table. "I've come to speak with you, Samuel, but you're all welcome to stay." He acknowledged David and Daniel.

"What is it?" asked Samuel anxiously.

George swallowed hard and announced, "I'd like to go to Cove Forge with you, if the invitation still stands."

Samuel leapt up and grasped George's broad forearms. "It's the answer to my prayers, George. I can't tell you how happy I am that you'll be coming along."

"Thank you, Samuel," George said. "I believe it's what Polly . . ." His voice quivered slightly. He coughed, shook his head slightly and looked directly at Samuel. "Polly would have wanted me to get on with things. She was all about living. Even if the Lord took her life, she'd have my hide if I give up on mine. But I need to sort things out – get a fresh start. Like you said, Samuel, in a place where Polly and our son can rest in peace in my mind. Where everything I see doesn't remind me of the past."

"We'll be missing a fine man when you leave," said Daniel, "but I believe it's a wise choice you're making. You're young and strong with many years ahead of you. You need to begin a new life, whatever it takes."

"Our 'brother' returned," said David in a rare sensitive moment that somewhat startled Samuel and his father. Catching their reaction, he added a bit more stoically, "It'll be fine to still have you close to the family."

"You've all been so kind," said George. "I hope to live up to your goodness. But, I've got lots to do before I leave." He looked at Samuel. "When are you planning to head back to Huntingdon County?"

"In about a week," Samuel answered. "But we can wait until you're set, if need be. What can we do to help?"

"I've actually begun sorting through in my mind what needs to be done. The house will sell as soon as I give the word. Abraham Lehman's been searching for a place ever since he and Doris Snowberger announced their engagement last week. Thought he'd do a back flip when I mentioned it to him."

"It's a fine house. I'm not surprised," said Daniel.

"Should be able to fit the goods I'd like to take along into a small spring wagon. I only have one question for Samuel about that."

"Yes, George?"

"About Polly's *kist*. I was hoping that you and Sarah might accept it for your little Jane."

A brief moment of poignant silence followed. Everyone knew how Polly had cherished her marriage chest.

"We'd be honored, George," said Samuel.

"I'm leaving all of the household goods that are inside for Elizabeth. Polly always fretted so about Elizabeth not paying enough mind to filling her *kist*. And the two of them had a special friendship. Besides, Jane will want to have her *own* linens and pots inside."

All four men nodded. George moved to the door and donned his hat confidently. "Then a week from today it is. At dawn, I'd guess?" He looked to Samuel for confirmation which he gave with another nod.

"God be with you," said Daniel extending his hand.

"I suppose we'll see," said George. "But having the Royers with me is a fine start."

The chirping crickets offered a soothing counterpoint to the creaking of the rocking chair as Catherine sat by the parlor window in the twilight with her newest grandchild asleep on her shoulder. The faintest puffs of warm air from baby Jane's wee nose tickled Catherine's neck and granted her spirit pure contentment. *So tiny, so trusting. Such a gift from God.*

She thought about the letter from John that was tucked in her apron pocket and smiled. *Sweet John. Your heart's lighter now.* She recalled his writing, '*Though I miss you every day, I am closer to God here in the mountains.*' Sarah had handed the message to Catherine and said, 'He smiles nearly every day now.'

Catherine thought about the ten *Taufscheine* stored in the carved wooden box on the secretary desk by the hallway arch – a record of each child she had been blessed to raise. She pictured the black ribbon she had tied around Polly's. *I pray that she's holding her babe in Heaven just as I'm holding this dear one.* Her vision wavered as she fought tranquil tears . . . *and that God is holding my dear Polly.*

Daniel paused as he passed through the front hallway on the way to his office. He studied his wife of 25 years rocking the beloved infant. *Where has time taken us? The joy and the pain – she's been with me. Gelobt sei Gott for my Catherine.* He went on by without disturbing her.

The early morning sun shining over the Blue Ridge Mountains to the east blinked through the patchwork of brilliant leaves that arched the front lane. As their small wagon reached the end and turned onto the road to town and the farther journey to Cove Forge, Sarah and Samuel waved farewell one last time. The family watched them disappear in silence. Anything said would only make the parting more difficult. Even Cate was at a loss for a comforting phrase.

Daniel removed his hat and ran his fingers through his shock of salt-and-pepper hair. He replaced the hat firmly and announced, "Sun's going to be plenty hot today. Don't want to miss the cooler morning hours. Second stand of flax needs to be pulled and laid in the stream." He headed for the barn, while Jacob made his way toward the mill and David to the tannery.

Catherine smoothed her apron and coughed to steady her voice. "Last of the cabbage needs shredded and brined. Girls, get to your chores."

"Yes, Mama," they answered.

Catherine took Nan's tiny hand. "Well, little one, how about we go to the summer kitchen to get started on noon meal and chop some cabbage. I think there might be a Johnnycake left from breakfast." The toddler smiled up at her mother as they made their way along the path.

As Catherine inspected the bread for mold that was so troublesome in warm humid weather, Nan studied the glass flycatcher on the plank table. Once the pests flew inside the openings at the bottom of the jar to feed on the tiny bowl of honey inside, they couldn't get out. Watching them buzz and flit around frantically inside the trap kept the child amused while Catherine stoked the fire to warm a kettle of stew. Sweat dripped from her brow as she leaned over to stir the mixture. "It might be hot, but we've still got to eat."

Susan and Rebecca pulled on their stiff leather work gloves as they headed for the four-square garden. No need to feel for hidden vegetables with bare fingers today. They would be pulling the spent stalks and vines and dragging them to the growing compost pile.

 They opened the whitewashed picket gate and plodded toward the mass of curling brown-tipped leaves in the raised bed at the far end. As they passed the center of the garden, the cross path marked by the Crown of Thorns shrub, Susan stopped. Rebecca continued a few steps before she missed her sister and then looked back.

"Come here." Susan beckoned with her hand.

"What?" Rebecca said furrowing her brow.

"Come back to the center," Susan repeated.

Rebecca moved beside her.

Susan smiled and took Rebecca's hands as they faced each other. "Now, just stand here a minute and look around – slowly." They both turned their heads as far as they could in either direction and then looked at each other. "Did you feel it?" Susan asked.

"Feel what?"

"The world slow down – things settle into place."

Rebecca shook her head. "What things?"

"This garden, the trees, the stream – doing the same thing, the *very* same thing they do every year. Each ending is a beginning and each beginning happens time after time – *every* year."

Rebecca didn't respond.

Susan dropped Rebecca's hands and ran to a bed of dying plants. Yanking one out, she shook the dirt from the roots and held up the stalk. "Look. This squash plant is dead. It may be droopy and sad, but the compost pile will welcome it and transform it into loam for the soil." She stooped down and grabbed a fistful of ground. "And next spring, like always, a new plant will grow new squash." Rebecca frowned, still not comprehending.

Susan stood and pointed to the kaleidoscope of trees along the nearby stream and around the stone house. "The autumn leaves are dying, but their beautiful offering will finally drop to the ground and crumble to feed the new green leaves next spring." She looked at Rebecca's face for a sign of recognition – a sign that she finally understood.

 She grinned as Rebecca's eyes began to widen and gleam. "The change – the *change* – it's always the same!" Rebecca exclaimed.

Susan came back and took Rebecca's hands again. "So many things are changing for us right now. I couldn't keep up with the sense of it all. The harder I tried, the sadder I got. Then something at the cross path today made me stop and look around, not *inside* at myself, but *outside* at the world and I suddenly felt some peace."

Rebecca looked around again and squeezed Susan's hands as their eyes met. "Like the scripture?" Rebecca asked. "*To everything there is a season, and a time to every purpose under heaven.*"

"Yes," said Susan. They hugged. "Yes," she repeated. They stared at the stone house, the place that finally felt like home – the anchor for their family. "And like Mama told me years ago when we left our old cabin – changed homes – when I was so upset. She said, '*Cherish the past. Anticipate the future. Embrace the present moment. Give God reverence always.*'

Threads of Change

Recipes for Featured Dishes

Chicken and Corn Soup (with rivels)

1 chicken (approx. 4 lbs.)	¼ cup shredded carrot
4 quarts cold water	10 ears of corn
1 medium chopped onion	2 hard-boiled eggs
½ cup chopped celery and leaves	salt and pepper to taste

Cook chicken until it is tender, adding salt 30 minutes before it is done.

Remove chicken and take meat from bones. Chop and add to broth.

Cut corn from cob and add to broth

Add chopped celery, onion, carrot and seasoning.

Ten minutes before serving, add 2 chopped hard boiled eggs and rivels made from:

> 1 cup flour
> 1 egg
> ¼ cup milk

Rub this mixture together with 2 forks until blended and drop by small bits into boiling soup.

Cover and boil for 7 minutes.   Serves 10

Shoo Fly Pie

Bottom Part:	Top Part:
¾ cup molasses (or dark Karo)	1 ½ cups flour
¾ cup boiling water	¼ cup shortening
½ teaspoon soda	½ cup brown sugar
pastry for 1 (9-inch) crust	

Dissolve soda in hot water and add molasses.

Combine sugar and flour and rub in shortening to make crumbs.

Pour 1/3 of liquid into unbaked crust.

Add 1/3 of crumb mixture.

Continue to alternate layers, putting crumbs on top.

Bake at 375 degrees for 35 minutes.

Pennsylvania Dutch Chicken Pot Pie (Bott Boi)

1 chicken (approx. 4 lbs.)
1 teaspoon salt
water to cover in 4-quart pot
4 medium potatoes, sliced
2 tablespoons chopped parsley

For pot pie dough:
2 cups flour
½ teaspoon salt
2 eggs
2-3 tablespoons water

In 4-quart pan, cook chicken in simmering water with salt until tender, about 1 hour.
   While chicken cooks, make pot pie dough:
      Make a well in flour and add eggs and salt.
      Work together into a stiff dough: if too dry, add water or milk.
      Roll out dough as thin as possible (1/8 inch) and cut into 1-inch squares.
      Coat pieces well with flour to keep separate until added to liquid.
Remove chicken and take meat from bones when cool. Discard skin and cut meat into bite-size pieces.
Bring broth to boil. Add chicken meat and sliced potatoes. Make sure liquid covers chicken well.
Gradually add the pot pie dough squares into the boiling liquid. Cook 10-12 minutes.
Add chopped parsley.   Serves 6 – 8

Sauerkraut with Sweet Potatoes

2 lbs. sauerkraut
1 large chopped onion
1 large sweet potato, cut in quarters
1 tart apple, cut in quarters

2 cups water
½ cup brown sugar
pepper to taste

Drain sauerkraut and place in large pot with remaining ingredients with water half-way up the mixture.
Bring to boil.
Reduce heat, cover and simmer until tender, at least 60 minutes.

Serves 4 – 6 as side dish.

Fried Sausage with Milk Gravy

1 lb. fresh link country sausage
2 tablespoons flour

1 cup milk
salt and pepper to taste

Cut sausage into desired pieces. Place in frying pan with a little water.
Bring to boil over low heat. Reduce heat and cover until sausage is cooked.
Remove lid and continue cooking over medium heat until water evaporates and sausage browns on all sides. Remove sausage from pan.
Add flour to pan drippings.
Gradually add milk stirring vigorously to prevent lumps as it thickens while scraping all from the browned bits in the bottom of the pan.
Add salt and pepper and serve with sausage.

*note – The Pennsylvania Dutch make milk gravy quite often, even without meat, using just bacon grease for flavoring. They will often add chunks of bread.

Hot Cabbage Slaw

1 quart shredded cabbage
1 teaspoon salt
2 tablespoons sugar
2 tablespoons vinegar

½ cup water
2 tablespoons butter
½ teaspoon mustard
½ cup sour cream

Melt the butter in a saucepan and add shredded cabbage.
Stir until butter is well mixed through the cabbage.
Add water and salt and cover tightly.
Cook for 10 minutes and then add the sugar, vinegar and mustard.
Simmer another minute and then add the sour cream.

Serves 4.

Spätzel with Browned Butter (German Noodles/Dumplings)

2 ½ cups flour   1 cup milk
¼ teaspoon salt   5 tablespoons butter
¼ teaspoon nutmeg   salt and pepper to taste
2 large eggs, beaten

Mix together flour, salt and nutmeg in large bowl.
Add egg and milk stirring until thoroughly combined
Let dough rest for about 15 minutes before cooking.
Heat large pot of water until boiling.
Put mixture, a quarter at a time, into colander and push through the holes into boiling water.
Cook about 4 minutes or until the dough floats.
Brown butter in a medium skillet and add the drained spaetzel, salt and pepper.
Toss to combine well and serve immediately.

Serves 4 as a side dish   * note – may be added to soups

Yeast

1 pint of hops   1 teaspoon salt
1 cup flour   3 lbs. potatoes, boiled and finely
1 cup sugar   mashed

Boil one pint of hops in 2 gallons of water.
Cool and strain.
Add flour, sugar and salt. (No yeast needed to require it to rise.)
Let stand 3 days in warm place until it begins to foam.
Boil potatoes, mash fine and add to the yeast stirring well.
Put mixture in tightly sealed container and set in cool place.
½ cup is sufficient for 6 loaves of bread.

* note - It should be made 2 weeks before using.

Glossary

abide	-	to tolerate, to bear
accommodate	-	to adjust
accumulate	-	to heap or pile up
accusatory	-	blaming, charging with a fault
acute	-	marked by keen discernment; critical, crucial
adjacent	-	nearby, beside
adjournment	-	ending a session or meeting
advent	-	the coming or arrival
alienation	-	loss of affection for someone or something
amble	-	to walk with ease
andirons	-	pair of metal supports for wood in a fireplace
animated	-	full of spirit
aspirant	-	one who desires to earn a worthy place
assess	-	to determine the importance, size or value of
assimilation	-	becoming part of a group or system
aura	-	an sense of light surrounding something
awestruck	-	filled with fearful wonder or respect
baffles (n.)	-	screens to regulate flow in a butter churn
banking	-	depending or counting on
bearings	-	sense of one's position or situation
belch	-	a loud burp
bodice	-	upper front part of a woman's dress or blouse
boisterous	-	full of high spirits and noise
breach	-	to break or violate

brine (v.)	-	to tear or soak with strong salt water
brogue	-	a regional accent or pronunciation
brood (v.)	-	to dwell on a subject; to be depressed
bulbous	-	swollen, resembling a bulb
buttress (v.)	-	to provide a support
calloused	-	having no sympathy; hard, thick-skinned
carcass	-	a dead body
celibate (n.)	-	one who decides to lived unmarried
chaff	-	the hard covering of grain seeds
clamor (v.)	-	to insist loudly on something
claustrophobia	-	a fear of being in closed or narrow spaces
cloister	-	a house for persons under religious vows
comely	-	pretty, pleasing
communal	-	used or shared in common with others
compost	-	mixture of decayed matter used as fertilizer
concoction	-	a combination of materials
conniption	-	a fit of alarm or rage
conspiratorial	-	having a plot against someone or something
contours	-	curving or irregular outline
cooperage	-	a business that produces wooden barrels
copse	-	a group of trees or high brush
cord	-	a stack of cut wood measuring 4x4x8 feet
corral (v.)	-	to gather or enclose
crane (v.)	-	to stretch one's neck to see better
crochet	-	needlework with interlocking looped stitches
crow (v.)	-	to boast or brag

defer	-	to put off or delay
devoid	-	without, completely empty
diligence	-	steady, earnest effort
disdain (v.)	-	to look on with scorn
disembark	-	to get out of a vehicle or ship
distorted	-	twisted out of shape
distraught	-	upset or agitated
doldrums	-	a slump, a spell of inactivity
dollop	-	a blob or lump
douse	-	to drench or extinguish with water
dubious	-	doubtful, full of misgivings
dumbstruck	-	made silent by surprise or astonishment
Dutch oven	-	cast-iron kettle with tight cover
ecstatic	-	overwhelmingly delighted or pleased
eddy	-	a small whirlpool
edict	-	a publicly announced law or decree
embers	-	hot coals or smoldering remains of a fire
engrossed	-	completely occupied or absorbed
entrails	-	internal organs
entwined	-	wrapped around
envelop (v.)	-	enclose or cover completely
escalate	-	to increase or expand
ethereal	-	heavenly; extremely delicate
evoke	-	to call forth or summon
exacted	-	demanded
exuberance	-	extreme enthusiasm

falter	-	to stumble or give way
fast (v.)	-	to go without food for a lengthy time
fervently	-	with great warmth or passion
floss	-	thread or yarn
footfalls	-	steps
fume (v.)	-	to have great irritation or anger
gauze	-	very thin, loosely woven fabric
giddiness	-	lightheartedness; foolishness
gnarled	-	twisted, distorted, misshapen
grate (v.)	-	to irritate
grimace (v.)	-	frown; scowl
grizzled	-	streaked with gray
harbinger	-	something that foreshadows what is to come
hatchel	-	heavy metal comb to separate fibers of flax
hewn	-	cut roughly by an ax or hatchet
homage	-	honor; respectful tribute
homespun	-	rough fabric made of wool or linen
hominy	-	shell of corn kernel with inner seed removed
hornbook	-	child's early school book, one covered page
immersed	-	covered in water or a fluid
impending	-	about to happen
imperative	-	order; command
infatuation	-	extreme love or affection, often foolish
influx	-	a flowing into
infuse	-	to instill a principle or quality
inquisition	-	a severe questioning

intone	-	to recite or say in singing tones
intrusive	-	entering when uninvited
Johnnycakes	-	flat bread of cornmeal, flour, eggs and milk
jubilation	-	great joy
kaleidoscope	-	a changing pattern or scene
kiln	-	oven for processing at very high temperatures
kindling	-	small sticks and brush used to start a fire
laden	-	loaded, burdened
lanky	-	tall and thin
lanolin	-	wool grease
leach	-	to soak in water to separate compounds
leathered	-	toughened, like leather
ledgers	-	books of accounts of payments and debts
leech	-	a bloodsucking worm once used by doctors
lethargic	-	lazy, indifferent
limb	-	arm or leg; primary branch of a tree
Lobsterback	-	a British soldier
magenta	-	deep, purplish red
meringue	-	fluffy white mixture of egg whites and sugar
meticulously	-	very carefully with great attention to detail
mire	-	deep mud
musing (n.)	-	deep thought
muster	-	to bring together; rally
muted	-	softened
nuptials	-	marriage ceremony
obliged	-	morally or legally bound

onslaught	-	a fierce attack
opt	-	choose
pallor	-	paleness
paralysis	-	inability to move
paraphernalia	-	collection of varying possessions or goods
pare (v.)	-	to peel or remove the outer covering
parchment	-	fine paper made of the skin of a sheep or goat
patriarch	-	the father or founder
pelt (v.)	-	to hit or beat repeatedly
penance	-	an act of devotion performed to repent for sin
pious	-	devout, marked by a devotion to God or faith
poultice	-	large medicated patch to treat illness
privy	-	outhouse
prodigious	-	extraordinary
proposal	-	suggestion; an offer of marriage
prospective	-	expected in the future
prosperity	-	economic success or well-being; wealth
protrude	-	to stick out
pulverize	-	to grind into small pieces or dust
pummel	-	to hit repeatedly
pungent	-	having a strong odor
quarry (v.)	-	to gather stone by digging or cutting
quill	-	large, stiff feather
quip	-	joke or jest
rambunctious	-	full of unruly energy
rasher	-	a portion of bacon or ham

recitation	-	speech or oral presentation
reel in (v.)	-	to draw closer with a winding motion
relent	-	to soften or give in
relinquish	-	to give up something desirable
remedy (n.)	-	cure; treatment
render	-	to make or cause to become
replenish	-	to replace or refill
repose	-	to rest or remain
reprieve	-	to delay punishment or give relief
resonant	-	echoing; pleasant sounding
resolve (n.)	-	determination
respite	-	a time of rest or relief
resplendent	-	dazzling, splendid
reverberate	-	to echo
roost (v.)	-	to perch on a limb or pole
rousing	-	lively, exciting
sallow	-	unhealthy yellow or pale brown in color
sacrament	-	a sacred or holy act
sanctuary	-	a place of safety; a sacred or holy place
sassafras	-	an American tree related to the laurel family
saturate	-	to soak completely
scoff	-	to sneer or show contempt
scorched	-	darkened or singed by heat or burning
scythe	-	a sharp, long-handled tool for cutting
seethe	-	to hold anger inside
sheaves	-	stalks of grain bound together in a bundle

shimmy	-	to shake or quiver
shorn	-	cut down or harvested
shun	-	to avoid deliberately and completely
silhouette	-	the outline of a dark or blackened object
smolder	-	to burn slowly; to suppress anger or hate
snitzen	-	cut pieces of raw apple
sobering	-	serious; causing serious thought or reaction
spellbound	-	fascinated
staunchly	-	strongly; faithfully
steep (v.)	-	to soak in a liquid
stern	-	severe
substantial	-	sturdy; important; true; full
succumb	-	to give into; to die
sumptuous	-	lavish; overflowing
survey (v.)	-	to examine or inspect
sustenance	-	nourishment
swath	-	a long strip left by cutting
sweltering	-	very hot
tableau	-	a picture or still scene
tandem	-	a group of two or more acting together
tangible	-	able to be seen or felt; real
tedious	-	dull, boring
temper (v.)	-	to control or soften
tentative	-	hesitant; uncertain
tenuous	-	weak; thin
tiff	-	a minor quarrel

till (v.)	-	cultivate; to work soil by raising crops
timely	-	coming at the right or appropriate time
tinge	-	to stain or affect the color of something
tome	-	a large, heavy book
torturous	-	very difficult; cruelly painful
traipse	-	to wander aimlessly
translucent	-	partly transparent; shining or glowing
tureen	-	a deep serving bowl
unscathed	-	not injured or harmed
upheaval	-	great change
utopian	-	perfect
vials	-	small bottles
ventilate	-	allow the flow of fresh air
vermin	-	small, disgusting animals
vibrant	-	full of life, vigor and activity
vigil	-	a constant, devoted watch or caring for
vulnerable	-	easily hurt or damaged
wary	-	cautious
wracked	-	tortured
wrenching	-	causing suffering or anguish
wretched	-	unhappy; miserable

9/15

20599365R00167

Made in the USA
San Bernardino, CA
16 April 2015